Veronika Decides to Die

ALSO BY PAULO COELHO

The Alchemist
The Pilgrimage
The Valkyries
By the River Piedra I Sat Down and Wept
The Fifth Mountain

PAULO COELHO

VERONIKA DECIDES TO DIE

TRANSLATED FROM THE PORTUGUESE
BY MARGARET JULL COSTA

HarperCollins *Publishers* India

HarperCollins *Publishers* India Pvt Ltd
7/16 Ansari Road, Daryaganj, New Delhi 110 002

First Published in English by
HarperCollins *Publishers*, U.K., 1999

First Published in India by
HarperCollins *Publishers* India 2000

ISBN 0 7225 3992 4

Printed in India by
Gopsons Papers Ltd
A-14 Sector 60
Noida 201 301

Behold I give unto you power to tread
on serpents ... and nothing shall by
any means hurt you.

Luke 10:19

For S.T. de L, who began to help me without my realising it.

On 11 November 1997, Veronika decided that the moment to kill herself had – at last! – arrived. She carefully cleaned·the room that she rented in a convent, turned off the heating, brushed her teeth and lay down.

She picked up the four packs of sleeping pills from her bedside table. Instead of crushing them and mixing them with water, she decided to take them one by one, because there is always a gap between intention and action, and she wanted to feel free to turn back half way. However, with each pill she swallowed, she felt more convinced: after five minutes the packs were empty.

Since she didn't know exactly how long it would take her to lose consciousness, she had placed on the bed that month's issue of a French magazine, *Homme*, which had just arrived in the library where she worked. She had no particular interest in computer science, but, as she leafed through the magazine, she came across an article about a computer game (one of those CD-Roms), created by Paulo Coelho, a Brazilian writer she had happened to meet at a lecture in the café at the Grand Union Hotel. They had exchanged a few words and she had ended up being invited by his publisher to join them for supper. There were a lot of people there, though, and they hadn't had a chance to talk in depth about anything.

The fact that she had met the author, however, led her to think that he was part of her world, and that reading an article about his work could help pass the time. While she was waiting for death, Veronika started reading about computer science, a subject in which she was not in the least bit interested, but then that was in keeping with what she had done all her life, always looking for the easy option, for whatever was nearest to hand. Like that magazine, for example.

To her surprise, though, the first line of text shook her out of her natural passivity (the tranquillizers had not yet dissolved in her stomach, but Veronika was, by nature, passive), and, for the first time in her life, it made her ponder the truth of a saying that was very fashionable amongst her friends: 'nothing in this world happens by chance'.

Why that first line, at precisely the moment when she had begun to die? What was the hidden message she saw before her, assuming there are such things as hidden messages rather than mere coincidences.

Underneath an illustration of the computer game, the journalist began his article by asking: 'Where is Slovenia?'

'Honestly,' she thought, 'no one ever knows where Slovenia is.'

But Slovenia existed nonetheless, and it was outside, inside, in the mountains around her and in the square she was looking out at: Slovenia was her country.

She put the magazine to one side, there was no point now in getting indignant with a world that knew absolutely nothing about the Slovenes; her nation's honour no longer concerned her. It was time to feel proud of herself, to recognise that she had been able to do this, that she had finally had the courage and was leaving this life: what joy! Also she was doing it as she had always dreamed she would – by taking sleeping pills, which leave no mark.

Veronika had been trying to get hold of the pills for nearly six months. Thinking that she would never manage it, she had even considered slashing her wrists. It didn't matter that the room would end up awash with blood, and the nuns would be left feeling confused and troubled, for suicide demands that people think of themselves first and of others later. She was prepared to do all she could so that her death would cause as little upset as possible, but if slashing her wrists was the only way, then she had no option – and the nuns could clean up the room and quickly forget the whole story, otherwise they would find it hard to rent out the room again. We may live at the end of the twentieth century, but people still believe in ghosts.

Obviously she could have thrown herself off one of the few tall buildings in Ljubljana, but what about the further suffering caused to her parents by a fall from such a height? Apart from the shock of learning that their daughter had died, they would also have to identify a disfigured corpse; no, that was a worse solution than bleeding to death, because it would leave indelible marks on two people who only wanted the best for her.

'They would get used to their daughter's death eventually. But it must be impossible to forget a shattered skull.'

Shooting, jumping off a high building, hanging, none of these options suited her feminine nature. Women, when they kill themselves, choose far more romantic methods – like slashing their wrists or taking an overdose of sleeping pills. Abandoned princesses and Hollywood actresses have provided numerous examples of this.

Veronika knew that life was always a matter of waiting for the right moment to act. And so it proved. In response to her complaints that she could no longer sleep at night, two friends of hers managed to get hold of two packs each of a powerful drug, used by musicians at a local nightclub. Veronika left the four packs on her bedside table for a week, courting approaching death and saying goodbye – entirely unsentimentally – to what people called Life.

Now she was there, glad she had gone all the way, and bored because she didn't know what to do with the little time that remained to her.

She thought again about the absurd question she had just read. How could an article about computers begin with such an idiotic opening line: 'Where is Slovenia?'

Having nothing more interesting to do, she decided to read the whole article and she learned that the said computer game had been made in Slovenia – that strange country that no one seemed quite able to place, except the people who lived there – because it was a cheap source of labour. A few months before, when the product was launched, the French manufacturer had given a party for journalists from all over the world in a castle in Vled.

Veronika remembered reading something about the party, which had been quite an event in the city, not just because the castle had been redecorated in order to match as closely as possible the medieval atmosphere of the CD-Rom, but because of the controversy in the local press: journalists from Germany, France, Britain, Italy and Spain had been invited, but not a single Slovene.

Homme's correspondent – who was visiting Slovenia for the first time, doubtless with all expenses paid, and determined to spend his visit chatting up other journalists, making supposedly interesting comments and enjoying the free food and drink at the castle – had decided to begin his article with a joke which must have appealed to the sophisticated intellectuals of his country. He had probably told his fellow journalists on the magazine various untrue stories about local customs too, and said how badly Slovene women dress.

That was *his* problem. Veronika was dying, and she had other concerns, such as wondering if there was life after death, or when her body would be found. Nevertheless – or perhaps precisely because of the important decision she had taken – the article bothered her.

She looked out of the convent window that gave on to the small square in Ljubljana. 'If they don't know where Slovenia is, then Ljubljana must be a myth,' she thought. Like Atlantis or Lemuria, or the other lost continents that fill men's imaginations. No one, anywhere in the world, would begin an article asking where Mount Everest was, even if they had never been there. Yet, in the middle of Europe, a journalist on an important magazine felt no shame at asking such a question, because he knew that most of his readers would not know where Slovenia was, still less its capital, Ljubljana.

It was then that Veronika found a way of passing the time, now that ten minutes had gone by and she had still not noticed any bodily changes. The final act of her life would be to write a letter to the magazine, explaining that Slovenia was one of the five republics into which the former Yugoslavia had been divided.

The letter would be her suicide note. She would give no explanation of the real reasons for her death.

When they found her body, they would conclude that she had killed herself because a magazine did not know where her country was. She laughed to think of the controversy in the newspapers, with some for and some against her suicide committed in honour of her country's cause. And she was shocked by how quickly she could change her mind, since only moments before she had thought exactly the opposite, that the world and other geographical problems were no longer her concern.

She wrote the letter. That moment of good humour almost made her have second thoughts about the need to die, but she had already taken the pills, it was too l :⁻ to turn back.

Anyway, she had had such moments before and, besides, she was not killing herself because she was a sad, embittered woman, constantly depressed. She had spent many afternoons walking gaily along the streets of Ljubljana or gazing – from the window in her convent room – at the snow falling on the small square with its statue of the poet. Once, for almost a month, she had felt as if she were walking on air, all because a complete stranger, in the middle of that very square, had given her a flower.

She believed herself to be completely normal. Two very simple reasons lay behind her decision to die, and she was sure that, were she to leave a note explaining, many people would agree with her.

The first reason: everything in her life was the same and, once her youth was gone, it would be downhill all the way, with old age beginning to leave irreversible marks, the onset of illness, the departure of friends. She would gain nothing by continuing to live; indeed, the likelihood of suffering only increased.

The second reason was more philosophical: Veronika read the newspapers, watched TV, and she was aware of what was going on in the world. Everything was wrong, and she had no way of putting things right – that gave her a sense of complete powerlessness.

In a short while, though, she would have the final experience of her life, which promised to be very different: death. She wrote the letter to the magazine, then abandoned the topic, and concentrated on more pressing matters, more appropriate to what she was living, or, rather, dying, through at that moment.

She tried to imagine what it would be like to die, but failed to reach any conclusion.

Besides, there was no point worrying about that, for in a few minutes' time she would know.

How many minutes?

She had no idea. But she relished the thought that she was about to find out the answer to the question that everyone asked themselves: does God exist?

Unlike many people, this had not been the great inner debate of her life. Under the old Communist regime, the official line in schools had been that life ended with death and she had got used to the idea. On the other hand, her parents' generation and her grandparents' generation still went to church, said prayers and went on pilgrimages, and were utterly convinced that God listened to what they said.

At twenty-four, having experienced everything she could experience – and that was no small achievement – Veronika was almost certain that everything ended with death. That is why she had chosen suicide: freedom at last. Eternal oblivion.

In her heart of hearts, though, there was still a doubt: what if God did exist? Thousands of years of civilization had made of suicide a taboo, an affront to all religious codes: man struggles to survive, not to succumb. The human race must procreate. Society needs workers. A couple has to have a reason to stay together, even when love has ceased to exist, and a country needs soldiers, politicians and artists.

'If God exists, and I truly don't believe he does, he will know that there are limits to human understanding. He was the one who created this confusion in which there is poverty, injustice, greed and loneliness. He doubtless had the best of intentions, but the results have proved disastrous; if God exists, He will be generous with those creatures who chose to leave this Earth early, and he might even apologise for having made us spend time here.'

To hell with taboos and superstitions. Her devout mother would say: God knows the past, the present and the future. In that case, He had placed her in this world in the full knowledge that she would end up killing herself, and He would not be shocked by her actions.

Veronika began to feel a slight nausea, which became rapidly more intense.

In a few moments, she would no longer be able to concentrate on the square outside her window. She knew it was winter, it must have been about four o'clock in the afternoon, and the sun was setting fast. She knew that other people would go on living. At that moment, a young man passed her window and saw her, utterly unaware that she was about to die. A group of Bolivian musicians (where is Bolivia? why don't magazine articles ask that?) were playing in front of the statue of France Prešeren, the great Slovenian poet, who had made such a profound impact on the soul of his people.

Would she live to hear the end of that music drifting up from the square? It would be a beautiful memory of this life: the late afternoon, a melody recounting the dreams of a country on the other side of the world, the warm cosy room, the handsome young man passing by, full of life, who had decided to stop and was now standing looking up at her. She realised that the pills were beginning to take effect and that he was the last person who would see her.

He smiled. She returned his smile – she had nothing to lose. He waved; she decided to pretend she was looking at something else, the young man was going too far. Disconcerted, he continued on his way, forgetting that face at the window for ever.

But Veronika was glad to have felt desired by somebody one last time. She wasn't killing herself because of a lack of love. It wasn't because she felt unloved by her family, or had money problems or an incurable disease.

Veronika had decided to die on that lovely Ljubjlana afternoon, with Bolivian musicians playing in the square, with a young man passing by her window, and she was happy with what her eyes could see and her ears hear. She was even happier that she would not have to go on seeing those same things for another thirty, forty or fifty years, because they would lose all their originality and be transformed into the tragedy of a life in which everything repeats itself and where one day is exactly like another.

Her stomach was beginning to churn now and she was feeling very ill indeed. 'It's odd, I thought an overdose of tranquillizers would send me straight to sleep.' What she was experiencing, though, was a strange buzzing in her ears and a desire to vomit.

'If I throw up, I won't die.'

She decided not to think about the stabbing pains in her stomach and tried to concentrate on the rapidly falling night, on the Bolivians, on the people who were starting to shut up their shops and go home. The noise in her ears was becoming more and more strident and, for the first time since she had taken the pills, Veronika felt fear, a terrible fear of the unknown.

It did not last long. Soon afterwards, she lost consciousness.

When she opened her eyes, Veronika did not think 'this must be heaven'. Heaven would never use a fluorescent tube to light a room, and the pain – which started a fraction of a second later – was typical of the Earth. Ah, that Earth pain – unique, unmistakable.

She tried to move and the pain increased. A series of bright dots appeared, but, even so, Veronika knew that those dots were not the stars of Paradise, but the consequences of the intense pain she was feeling.

'She's coming round,' she heard a woman say. 'You've landed slap bang in hell, so you'd better make the most of it.'

No, it couldn't be true, that voice was deceiving her. It wasn't hell, because she felt really cold and she was aware of plastic tubes coming out of her nose and mouth. One of the tubes – the one stuck down her throat – made her feel as if she were choking.

She made as if to remove it, but her arms were strapped down.

'I'm joking, it's not really hell,' the voice went on. 'It's worse than hell, not that I've ever actually been there. You're in Villete.'

Despite the pain and the feeling of choking, Veronika realised at once what had happened. She had tried to kill herself and someone had arrived in time to save her. It could have been one of the nuns, a friend who had decided to drop by unannounced, someone delivering something she had forgotten she had ordered. The fact is, she had survived, and she was in Villete.

Villete, the famous and much-feared lunatic asylum, which had been in existence since 1991, the year of the country's independence. At that time, believing that the partitioning of the former Yugoslavia would be achieved through peaceful means (after all, Slovenia had only experienced eleven days of war), a group of European businessmen had obtained permission to set up a hospital for mental patients in an old barracks, abandoned because of high maintenance costs.

Shortly afterwards, however, the wars commenced: first in Croatia, then in Bosnia. The businessmen were worried. The money for the investment came from capitalists scattered all round the globe, from people whose names they didn't even know, so there was no possibility of sitting down in front of them, offering a few excuses and asking them to be patient. They resolved the problem by adopting practices which were far from commendable in a psychiatric hospital, and for the young nation that had just emerged from a benign communism, Villete came to symbolise all the worst aspects of capitalism: to be admitted to the hospital, all you needed was money.

There was no shortage of people who, in their desire to get rid of some family member because of arguments over an inheritance (or over that person's embarrassing behaviour), were willing to pay large sums of money to obtain a medical report that would allow the internment of their problematic children or parents. Others, fleeing from debts or trying to justify certain attitudes that could otherwise result in long prison sentences, spent a brief time in the asylum and then simply left without paying any penalty or undergoing any judicial process.

Villete was the place from which no one had ever escaped, where genuine madmen – sent there by the courts or by other hospitals – mingled with those merely accused of madness or those pretending to be mad. The result was utter confusion, and the press were constantly publishing tales of ill-treatment and abuse, although they had never been given permission to visit Villete and actually see what was happening. The government was investigating the complaints, but could get no proof; the shareholders threatened to spread the word that foreign investment was difficult in Slovenia, and so the institution managed to remain afloat, indeed, it went from strength to strength.

'My aunt killed herself a few months ago,' the female voice continued. 'For almost eight years she was too afraid to even leave her room, eating, getting fat, smoking, taking tranquillisers and sleeping most of the time. She had two daughters and a husband who loved her.'

Veronika tried to move her head in the direction of the voice, but failed.

'I only saw her fight back once, when her husband took a lover. Then she kicked up a fuss, lost a few pounds, smashed some glasses and – for weeks on end – kept the rest of the whole neighbourhood awake with her shouting. Absurd though it may seem, I think that was the happiest time of her life. She was fighting for something, she felt alive and capable of responding to the challenges facing her.'

'What's all that got to do with me?' thought Veronika, unable to say anything. 'I'm not your aunt and I haven't got a husband.'

'In the end, her husband got rid of his lover,' said the woman, 'and gradually, my aunt returned to her former passivity. One day, she phoned to say that she wanted to change her life: she'd given up smoking. That same week, after increasing the number of tranquillisers she was taking because she'd stopped smoking, she told everyone that she wanted to kill herself.

'No one believed her. Then, one morning, she left a message on my answerphone, saying goodbye, and she gassed herself. I listened to that message several times: I had never heard her sound so calm, so resigned to her fate. She said she was neither happy nor unhappy, and that was why she couldn't go on.'

Veronika felt sorry for the woman telling the story, for she seemed to be doing so in an attempt to understand her aunt's death. In a world where everyone struggles to survive whatever the cost, how could one judge those people who decide to die?

No one can judge. Each person knows the extent of their own suffering, or the total absence of meaning in their lives. Veronika wanted to explain that, but instead she choked on the tube in her mouth and the woman hurried to her aid.

She saw the woman bending over her bound body, which was full of tubes and protected against her will, her freely expressed desire to destroy it. She moved her head from side to side, pleading with her eyes for them to remove the tubes and let her die in peace.

'You're upset,' said the woman. 'I don't know if you're sorry for what you did or if you still want to die; that doesn't interest me. What interests me is doing my job. If the patient gets agitated, the regulations say I must give them a sedative.'

Veronika stopped struggling, but the nurse was already injecting something into her arm. Soon afterwards, she was back in a strange dreamless world, where the only thing she could remember was the face of the woman she had just seen:

green eyes, brown hair, and a very distant air, the air of someone doing things because she has to do them, never questioning why the rules say this or that.

Paulo Coelho heard about Veronika's story three months later when he was having supper in an Algerian restaurant in Paris with a Slovenian friend, also called Veronika, who happened to be the daughter of the doctor in charge at Villete.

Later, when he decided to write a book about the subject, he considered changing his friend's name in order not to confuse the reader. He thought of calling her Blaska or Edwina or Marietzja, or some other Slovenian name, but he ended up keeping the real names. When he referred to his friend Veronika, he would call her his friend, Veronika. When he referred to the other Veronika, there would be no need to describe her at all, because she would be the central character in the book, and people would get irritated if they were always having to read 'Veronika the mad woman,' or 'Veronika the one who tried to commit suicide'. Besides, both he and his friend Veronika would only take up a very brief part of the book, this part.

His friend Veronika was horrified at what her father had done, especially bearing in mind that he was the director of an institution seeking respectability and was himself working on a thesis that would be judged by the conventional academic community.

'Do you know where the word "asylum" comes from?' she was saying. 'It dates back to the Middle Ages, from a person's

15

right to seek refuge in churches and other holy places. The right of asylum is something any civilised person can understand. So how could my father, the director of an asylum, treat someone like that?'

Paulo Coelho wanted to know all the details of what had happened, because he had a genuine reason for finding out about Veronika's story.

The reason was the following: he himself had been admitted into an asylum or, rather, mental hospital as they were better known. And this had happened not once, but three times, in 1965, 1966 and 1967. The place where he had been interned was the Dr Eiras Sanatorium in Rio de Janeiro.

Precisely why he had been admitted into hospital was something which, even today, he found odd; perhaps his parents were confused by his unusual behaviour, half-shy, half-extrovert, and by his desire to be an 'artist', something that everyone in the family considered a perfect recipe for ending up as a social outcast and dying in poverty.

When he thought about it – and, it must be said, he rarely did – he considered the real madman to have been the doctor who had agreed to admit him for the flimsiest of reasons (as in any family, the tendency is always to place the blame on others, and to state adamantly that the parents didn't know what they were doing when they took that drastic decision).

Paulo laughed when he learned of the strange letter to the newspapers that Veronika had left behind, complaining that an important French magazine didn't even know where Slovenia was.

'No one would kill themselves over something like that.'

'That's why the letter had no effect,' said his friend Veronika, embarrassed. 'Yesterday, when I checked in at the hotel, the receptionist thought Slovenia was a town in Germany.'

He knew the feeling, for many foreigners believed the Argentine city of Buenos Aires to be the capital of Brazil.

But apart from having foreigners blithely compliment him on the beauty of his country's capital city (which was to be found in the neighbouring country of Argentina), Paulo Coelho shared with Veronika the fact just mentioned, but which is worth restating: he too had been admitted into a mental hospital, and, as his first wife had once remarked, 'should never have been let out'.

But he was let out. And when he left the sanatorium for the last time, determined never to go back, he had made two promises: (a) that he would one day write about the subject and (b) that he would wait until both his parents were dead before touching publicly on the issue, because he didn't want to hurt them, since both had spent many years of their lives blaming themselves for what they had done.

His mother had died in 1993, but his father, who had turned eighty-four in 1997, was still alive and in full possession of his mental faculties and his health, despite having emphysema of the lungs (even though he'd never smoked) and despite living entirely off frozen food because he couldn't get a housekeeper who could put up with his eccentricities.

So, when Paulo Coelho heard Veronika's story, he discovered a way of talking about the issue without breaking his promises. Even though he had never considered suicide, he had an intimate knowledge of the world of the mental hospital – the treatments, the relationships between doctors and patients, the comforts and anxieties of living in a place like that.

So let us allow Paulo Coelho and his friend Veronika to leave this book for good and let us get on with the story.

Veronika didn't know how long she had slept. She remembered waking up at one point – still with the life-giving tubes in her mouth and nose – and hearing a voice say:

'Do you want me to masturbate you?'

But now, looking round the room with her eyes wide open, she didn't know if that had been real or an hallucination. Apart from that one memory, she could remember nothing, absolutely nothing.

The tubes had been taken out, but she still had needles stuck all over her body, wires connected to the area around her heart and her head, and her arms were still strapped down. She was naked, covered only by a sheet, and she felt cold, but she was determined not to complain. The small area surrounded by green curtains was filled by the bed she was lying on, the machinery of the Intensive Care Unit and a white chair on which a nurse was sitting reading a book.

This time, the woman had dark eyes and brown hair. Even so, Veronika was not sure if it was the same person she had talked to hours – or was it days? – ago.

'Can you unstrap my arms?'

The nurse looked up, said a brusque 'No', and went back to her book.

I'm alive, thought Veronika. Everything's going to start all

18

over again. I'll have to stay in here for a while, until they realise that I'm perfectly normal. Then they'll let me out, and I'll see the streets of Ljubljana again, its main square, the bridges, the people going to and from work.

Since people always tend to help others – just so that they can feel they are better than they really are – they'll give me my job back at the library. In time, I'll start frequenting the same bars and nightclubs, I'll talk to my friends about the injustices and problems of the world, I'll go to the cinema, take walks around the lake.

Since I only took sleeping pills, I'm not disfigured in any way: I'm still young, pretty, intelligent, I won't have any difficulty in getting boyfriends, I never did. I'll make love with them in their houses, or in the woods, I'll feel a certain degree of pleasure, but the moment I reach orgasm, the feeling of emptiness will return. We won't have much to talk about, and both he and I will know it. The time will come to make our excuses – 'It's late', or 'I have to get up early tomorrow' – and we'll part as quickly as possible, avoiding looking each other in the eye.

I'll go back to my rented room in the convent. I'll try and read a book, turn on the TV to see the same old programmes, set the alarm clock to wake up at exactly the same time I woke up the day before and mechanically repeat my tasks at the library. I'll eat a sandwich in the park opposite the theatre, sitting on the same bench, along with other people who also choose the same benches on which to sit and have their lunch, people who all have the same vacant look, but pretend to be pondering extremely important matters.

Then I'll go back to work, I'll listen to the gossip about who's going out with whom, who's suffering from what, how such and such a person was in tears about her husband, and I'll be left with the feeling that I'm privileged: I'm pretty, I have a job, I can have any boyfriend I choose. So I'll go back to the bars at the end of the day, and the whole thing will start again.

My mother, who must be out of her mind with worry over my suicide attempt, will recover from the shock and will keep asking me what I'm going to do with my life, why I'm not the same as everyone else, things really aren't as complicated as I think they are. 'Look at me, for example, I've been married to your father for years, and I've tried to give you the best possible upbringing and set you the best possible example.'

One day, I'll get tired of hearing her constantly repeating the same things, and to please her I'll marry a man whom I oblige myself to love. He and I will end up finding a way of dreaming of a future together: a house in the country, children, our children's future. We'll make love often in the first year, less in the second, and after the third year, people perhaps think about sex only once a fortnight and transform that thought into action only once a month. Even worse, we'll barely talk. I'll force myself to accept the situation, and I'll wonder what's wrong with me, because he no longer takes any interest in me, ignores me, and does nothing but talk about his friends, as if they were his real world.

When the marriage is just about to fall apart, I'll get pregnant. We'll have a child, feel closer to each other for a while, and then the situation will go back to what it was before.

I'll begin to put on weight like the aunt that nurse was talking about yesterday – or was it days ago, I don't really know. And I'll start to go on diets, systematically defeated each day, each week, by the weight that keeps creeping up regardless of the controls I put on it. At that point, I'll take those magic pills that stop you feeling depressed, then I'll have a few more children, conceived during nights of love that pass all too quickly.

I'll tell everyone that the children are my reason for living, when in reality my life is their reason for living.

People will always consider us a happy couple, and no one will know how much solitude, bitterness and resignation lies beneath the surface happiness.

Until one day, when my husband takes a lover for the first time, and I will perhaps kick up a fuss like the nurse's aunt, or think again of killing myself. By then, though, I'll be too old and cowardly, with two or three children who need my help, and I'll have to bring them up and help them find a place in the world before I can just abandon everything. I won't commit suicide: I'll make a scene, I'll threaten to leave and take the children with me. Like all men, my husband will back down, he'll tell me he loves me and that it won't happen again. It won't even occur to him that, if I really did decide to leave, my only option would be to go back to my parents' house and stay there for the rest of my life, forced to listen to my mother going on and on all day about how I lost my one opportunity for being happy, that he was a wonderful husband despite his peccadillos, that my children will be traumatised by the separation.

Two or three years later, another woman will appear in his life. I'll find out – because I saw them, or because someone told me – but this time I'll pretend I don't know. I used up all my energy fighting against that other lover, I've no energy left, it's best to accept life as it really is, and not as I imagined it to be. My mother was right.

He will continue being a considerate husband, I will continue working at the library, eating my sandwiches in the square opposite the theatre, reading books I never quite manage to finish, watching television programmes that are the same as they were ten, twenty, fifty years ago.

Except that I'll eat my sandwiches with a sense of guilt, because I'm getting fatter; and I won't go to bars any more, because I have a husband expecting me to come home and look after the children.

After that, it's a matter of waiting for the children to grow up and of spending all day thinking about suicide, without the courage to do anything about it. One fine day, I'll reach the conclusion that that's what life is like, there's no point worrying about it, nothing will change. And I'll accept it.

Veronika brought her interior monologue to a close and made a promise to herself: she would not leave Villete alive. It was best to put an end to everything now, while she was still brave and healthy enough to die.

She fell asleep and woke up several times, noticing that the number of machines around her was diminishing, the warmth of her body was growing, and the nurses' faces kept changing; but there was always someone beside her. Through the green curtain she heard the sound of someone crying, groans or voices whispering in calm, technical tones. From time to time, a distant machine would buzz and she would hear hurried foot-steps along the corridor. Then the voices would lose their calm, technical tone and become tense, issuing rapid orders.

In one of her lucid moments, a nurse asked her:

'Don't you want to know how you are?'

'I already know,' replied Veronika. 'And it's nothing to do with what you can see happening in my body, it's what's hap-pening in my soul.'

The nurse tried to continue the conversation, but Veronika pretended to be asleep.

When she opened her eyes again for the first time, she realised that she had been moved; she was in what looked like a large ward. She still had a drip in her arm, but all the other wires and needles had been removed.

A tall doctor, wearing the traditional white coat, in sharp contrast to the artificial black of his dyed hair and beard, was standing at the foot of her bed. Beside him, a young junior doctor holding a clipboard was taking notes.

'How long have I been here?' she asked, noticing that she spoke with some difficulty, slurring her words slightly.

'You've been in this ward for two weeks, after five days spent in the Intensive Care Unit,' replied the older man. 'And just be grateful that you're still here.'

The younger man seemed surprised, as if that final remark did not quite fit the facts. Veronika noticed his reaction at once, and her instincts were alerted: had she been here longer? Was she still in some danger? She began to pay attention to each gesture, each movement the two men made; she knew it was pointless asking questions, they would never tell her the truth, but if she was clever, she could find out what was going on.

'Tell me your name, address, marital status and date of birth,' the older man said. Veronika knew her name, her marital status and her date of birth, but she realised there were blanks

23

in her memory: she couldn't quite remember her address.

The doctor shone a light in her eyes and examined them for a long time, in silence. The young man did the same thing. They exchanged glances, which meant absolutely nothing.

'Did you say to the night nurse that we couldn't see into your soul?' asked the younger man.

Veronika couldn't remember. She was having difficulty knowing who she was and what she was doing there.

'You have been kept in an artificially induced sleep with tranquillisers, and that might affect your memory a bit, but please try to answer all our questions.'

And the doctors began an absurd questionnaire, wanting to know the names of the principal Ljubljana newspapers, the name of the poet whose statue was in the main square (ah, that she would never forget, every Slovene has the image of Prešeren engraved on his or her soul), the colour of her mother's hair, the names of her colleagues at work, the titles of the most popular books at the library.

To begin with, Veronika considered not replying – her memory was still confused – but as the questionnaire continued, she began reconstructing what she'd forgotten. At one point, she remembered that she was now in a mental hospital, and that the mad were not obliged to be coherent; but, for her own good, and to keep the doctors by her side, in order to see if she could find out something more about her state, she began making a mental effort. As she recited the names and facts, she was recovering not only her memory, but also her personality, her desires, her way of seeing life. The idea of suicide, which, that morning, appeared buried beneath several layers of sedatives, resurfaced.

'Fine,' said the older man, at the end of the questionnaire.

'How much longer must I stay here?'

The younger man lowered his eyes, and she felt as if everything were hanging in the air, as if, once that question was answered, a new chapter of her life would be written, and no one would be able to change it.

'You can tell her,' said the older man. 'A lot of other patients have already heard the rumours, and she'll find out in the end anyway; it's impossible to keep secrets round here.'

'Well, you decided your own fate,' sighed the young man, weighing each word. 'So you had better know the consequence of your actions: during the coma brought on by the pills you took, your heart was irreversibly damaged. There was a necrosis of the ventricle...'

'Put it in layman's terms,' said the older man. 'Get straight to the point.'

'Your heart was irreversibly damaged and soon it will stop beating altogether.'

'What does that mean?' she asked, frightened.

'If your heart stops beating, that means only one thing, death. I don't know what your religious beliefs are, but...'

'When will my heart stop beating?' asked Veronika, interrupting him.

'Within five days, a week at most.'

Veronika realised that behind his professional appearance and behaviour, behind the concerned manner, the young man was taking immense pleasure in what he was saying, as if she deserved the punishment, and would serve as an example to all the others.

During her life, Veronika had noticed that a lot of people she knew would talk about the horrors in other people's lives as if they were genuinely concerned to help them, but the truth was that they took pleasure in the suffering of others, because that made them believe they were happy and that life had been generous with them. She hated that kind of person and she wasn't going to give the young man an opportunity to take advantage of her state, in order to mask his own frustrations.

She kept her eyes fixed on his and, smiling, said:

'So I succeeded then.'

'Yes,' came the reply. But any pleasure he had taken in giving her the tragic news had vanished.

During the night, however, she began to feel afraid. It was one thing to die quickly after taking some pills, it was quite another to wait five days or a week for death to come, when she had already been through so much.

She had always spent her life waiting for something: for her father to come back from work, for the letter from a lover that never arrived, for her end-of-year exams, for the train, the bus, the phone call, the holiday, the end of the holidays. Now she was going to have to wait for death, which had made an appointment with her.

'This could only happen to me. Normally, people die on precisely the day they least expect.'

She had to get out of there and get some more pills. If she couldn't, and the only solution was to jump from a high building in Ljubljana, that's what she'd do; she had tried to save her parents any unnecessary suffering, but now she had no option.

She looked about her. All the beds were occupied by sleeping people, some of whom were snoring loudly. There were bars on the windows. At the end of the ward, there was a small bright light that filled the place with strange shadows and meant that the ward could be kept under constant vigilance. Near the light, a woman was reading a book.

'These nurses must be very cultivated, they spend their whole lives reading.'

Veronika's bed was the farthest from the door; between her and the woman there were nearly twenty other beds. She got up with difficulty because, if she was to believe what the doctor had said, she hadn't walked for nearly three weeks. The nurse looked up and saw the girl approaching, dragging her drip-feed with her.

'I want to go to the toilet,' she whispered, afraid of waking the other mad women.

The woman gestured vaguely towards the door. Veronika's mind was working fast, looking everywhere for an escape route, a crack, a way out. 'It has to be quick, while they think I'm still too frail, incapable of acting.'

She peered about her. The toilet was a cubicle with no door. If she wanted to get out of there, she would have to grab the nurse and overcome her in order to get the key from her, but she was too weak for that.

'Is this a prison?' she asked the nurse, who had stopped reading and was now watching her every movement.

'No, it's a mental hospital.'

'But I'm not mad.'

The woman laughed.

'That's what they all say.'

'All right then, I am mad, but what does that mean?'

The woman told Veronika not to stay too long on her feet, and sent her back to her bed.

'What does it mean to be mad?' insisted Veronika.

'Ask the doctor tomorrow. But go to sleep now, otherwise I'll have to give you a sedative, whether you want it or not.'

Veronika obeyed. On her way back, she heard someone whispering from one of the beds:

'Don't you know what it means to be mad?'

For a moment, she considered ignoring the voice: she didn't want to make friends, to develop a social circle, to create allies for a great mass revolt. She had only one fixed idea: death. If she really couldn't escape, she would find some way to kill herself right there, as soon as possible.

But the woman asked her the same question she had asked the nurse.

'Don't you know what it means to be mad?'

'Who are you?'

'My name is Zedka. Go to your bed. Then, when the nurse thinks you're asleep, crawl back over here.'

Veronika returned to her bed, and waited for the nurse to resume her reading. What did it mean to be mad? She hadn't the slightest idea, because the word was used in a completely anarchic way: people would say, for example, that certain sportsmen were mad because they wanted to break records, or that artists were mad, because they led such strange, insecure lives, different from the lives of normal people. On the other hand, Veronika had often seen thinly clad people walking the streets of Ljubljana in winter, pushing supermarket trolleys full of plastic bags and rags, and proclaiming the end of the world.

She didn't feel sleepy. According to the doctor, she had slept for almost a week, too long for someone who was used to a life without great emotions, but with rigid timetables for rest. What did it mean to be mad? Perhaps she should ask one of the mad.

Veronika crouched down, pulled the needle out of her arm and went over to Zedka's bed, trying to ignore her churning stomach. She didn't know if the feeling of nausea was because of her weakened heart or the effort she was having to make.

'I don't know what it means to be mad,' whispered Veronika. 'But I'm not. I'm just a failed suicide.'

'Anyone who lives in their own world is mad. Like schizo-phrenics, psychopaths, maniacs. I mean people who are differ-ent from others.'

'Like you?'

'On the other hand,' Zedka continued, pretending not to have heard the remark, 'you have Einstein, saying that there was no time or space, just a combination of the two. Or Columbus, insisting that on the other side of the world lay not an abyss but a continent. Or Edmund Hillary, convinced that a man could reach the top of Everest. Or the Beatles, who created an entirely different sort of music and dressed like people from another time. Those people – and thousands of others – all lived in their own world.'

'This madwoman talks a lot of sense,' thought Veronika, remembering stories her mother used to tell her about saints who swore they had spoken to Jesus or the Virgin Mary. Did *they* live in a world apart?

'I once saw a woman wearing a low-cut dress; she had a glazed look in her eyes and she was walking the streets of Ljubljana when it was five degrees below zero. I thought she must be drunk and I went to help her, but she refused my offer to lend her my jacket. Perhaps in her world it was summer and her body was warmed by the desire of the person waiting for her. Even if that person only existed in her delirium, she had the right to live and die as she wanted, don't you think?'

Veronika didn't know what to say, but the madwoman's words made sense to her. Who knows, perhaps she was the woman who had been seen half-naked walking the streets of Ljubljana?

'I'm going to tell you a story,' said Zedka. 'A powerful wiz-ard, who wanted to destroy an entire kingdom, placed a magic potion in the well from which all the inhabitants drank. Whoever drank that water would go mad.

'The following morning, the whole population drank from the well and they all went mad, apart from the king and his family, who had a well set aside for them alone, and which the magician had not managed to poison. The king was worried and tried to control the population by issuing a series of edicts governing security and public health. The policemen and the inspectors, however, had also drunk the poisoned water and they thought the king's decisions were absurd and resolved to take no notice of them.

'When the inhabitants of the kingdom heard these decrees, they became convinced that the king had gone mad and was now giving nonsensical orders. They marched on the castle and called for his abdication.

'In despair, the king prepared to step down from the throne, but the queen stopped him, saying: "Let us go and drink from the communal well. Then, we will be the same as them."

'And that was what they did: the king and the queen drank the water of madness and immediately began talking nonsense. Their subjects repented at once; now that the king was displaying such wisdom, why not allow him to continue ruling the country?

'The country continued to live in peace, although its inhabitants behaved very differently from those of its neighbours. And the king was able to govern until the end of his days.'

Veronika laughed.

'You don't seem mad at all,' she said.

'But I am, although I'm undergoing a cure, because my problem is that I lack a particular chemical. However, while I hope that the chemical gets rid of my chronic depression, I want to continue being mad, living my life the way I dream it, and not the way other people want it to be. Do you know what exists out there, beyond the walls of Villete?'

'People who have all drunk from the same well.'

'Exactly,' said Zedka. 'They think they're normal, because they all do the same thing. Well, I'm going to pretend that I have drunk from the same well as them.'

'I already did that, and that's precisely my problem. I've never been depressed, never felt great joy or sadness, at least none that lasted. I have the same problems as everyone else.'

For a while, Zedka said nothing, then:

'They told us you're going to die.'

Veronika hesitated for a moment. Could she trust this woman? She needed to take the risk.

'Yes, within about five or six days. I keep wondering if there's a way of dying sooner. If you, or someone else, could get me some more pills, I'm sure my heart wouldn't survive this time. You must understand how awful it is to have to wait for death, you must help me.'

Before Zedka could reply, the nurse appeared with an injection.

'I can give you the injection myself,' she said, 'or, depending on how you feel about it, I can ask the guards outside to help me.'

'Don't waste your energy,' said Zedka to Veronika. 'Save your strength, if you want to get what you asked me.'

Veronika got up, went back to her bed and allowed the nurse to do her work.

It was her first normal day in a mental hospital. She left the ward, had some breakfast in the large refectory where men and women were eating together. She noticed how different it was to the way these places were usually depicted in films – hysterical scenes, shouting, people making demented gestures – everything seemed wrapped in an aura of oppressive silence; it seemed that no one wanted to share their inner world with strangers.

After breakfast (which wasn't bad at all, no one could blame Villete's terrible reputation on the meals), they all went out to take the sun. In fact, there wasn't any sun – the temperature was below zero and the garden was covered in snow.

'I'm not here to preserve my life, but to lose it,' said Veronika to one of the nurses.

'You must still go out and take the sun.'

'You're the ones who are mad; there isn't any sun.'

'But there is light, and that helps to calm the patients. Unfortunately, our winter lasts a long time, if it didn't, we'd have a lot less work.'

It was useless arguing; she went out and walked a little, looking about her and surreptitiously seeking some way of escaping. The wall was high, as required by the builders of the old type of barracks, but the watchtowers for the sentries were empty. The garden was surrounded by military-looking buildings, which now housed the male and female wards, the administrative offices and the employees' rooms. After a first, rapid inspection, she noticed that the only place that was really guarded was the main gate, where everyone who entered and left had their papers checked by two guards.

Everything seemed to be falling into place in her mind again. In order to exercise her memory, she began trying to remember small things, like the place where she used to leave the key to her room, the record she'd just bought, the last book she was asked for at the library.

'I'm Zedka,' said a woman, approaching.

The previous night, Veronika hadn't been able to see her face, she had been crouched down beside the bed all the time they were talking. Zedka must have been about thirty-five and seemed absolutely normal.

'I hope the injection didn't bother you too much. After a while, the body gets habituated, and the sedatives lose their effect.'

'I'm fine.'

'About our conversation last night, do you remember what you asked me?'

'Of course I do.'

Zedka took her by the arm, and they began to walk along together, amongst the many leafless trees in the courtyard. Beyond the walls, you could see the mountains disappearing into the clouds.

'It's cold, but a lovely morning all the same,' said Zedka. 'Oddly enough, I never used to suffer from depression on cold, grey, cloudy days like this. I felt as if nature was in harmony with me, that it reflected my soul. On the other hand, when the sun appeared, the children would come out to play in the streets, and everyone was happy that it was such a lovely day, and then I would feel terrible, as if that display of exuberance in which I could not participate was somehow unfair.'

Delicately, Veronika detached herself from the woman. She didn't like physical contact.

'You didn't finish what you were saying. You were saying something about what I asked you last night.'

'There's a group of people here, men and women who could have left, who could be back home, but who don't want to leave. There are many reasons for this: Villete isn't as bad as people say, although it's far from being a five-star hotel. Here inside, everyone can say what they like, do what they want, without being criticised, after all, they're in a mental hospital. Then, when there are government inspections, these men and women behave like dangerous maniacs, because some are here at the State's expense. The doctors know this, but there must be some order from the owners which allows the situation to continue, because there are more vacancies than there are patients.'

'Could they get hold of some pills for me?'

'Try and contact them, they call their group the Fraternity.'

Zedka pointed to a woman with white hair, who was talking animatedly with some younger women.

'Her name is Mari, she belongs to the Fraternity. Ask her.'

Veronika started walking towards Mari, but Zedka stopped her:

'No, not now, she's having fun. She's not going to stop something which gives her pleasure, just to be nice to a complete stranger. If she should react badly, you'll never have another chance to approach her. The "mad" always believe in first impressions.'

Veronika laughed at the way Zedka said the word 'mad', but she was worried too, because everything here seemed so normal, so nice. After so many years of going straight from work to a bar, from that bar to the bed of some lover, from his bed to her room, from her room to her mother's house, she was now experiencing something she had never dreamed of:

35

a mental hospital, madness, an insane asylum, where people were not ashamed to say they were mad, where no one stopped doing something they were enjoying just to be nice to others.

She began to doubt that Zedka was serious, or if it wasn't just a way by which mental patients could pretend that the world they lived in was better than that of others. But what did it matter? She was experiencing something interesting, different, totally unexpected: imagine a place where people pretend to be mad in order to do exactly what they want.

At that precise moment, Veronika's heart turned over. She suddenly remembered what the doctor had said and she felt frightened.

'I want to walk alone for a bit,' she said to Zedka. After all, she was 'mad' too, and she no longer had to worry about pleasing anyone.

The woman moved off, and Veronika stood looking at the mountains beyond the walls of Villete. A faint desire to live seemed about to surface, but Veronika determinedly pushed it away.

'I must get hold of those pills as soon as possible.'

She reflected on her situation there; it was far from ideal. Even if they allowed her to do all the mad things she wanted to do, she wouldn't know where to start.

She had never done anything mad.

After some time in the garden, everyone went back to the refectory and had lunch. Immediately afterwards, the nurses led both men and women to a huge lounge divided up into lots of different areas; there were tables, chairs, sofas, a piano, a television and large windows through which you could see the grey sky and the low clouds. None of the windows had bars on them, because the room opened onto the garden. The doors were closed because of the cold, but all you had to do was turn the handle, and you could go outside again and walk once more amongst the trees.

Most people went and sat down in front of the television. Others stared into space, others talked in low voices to themselves, but who has not done the same at some moment in their lives? Veronika noticed that the older woman, Mari, was now with a larger group, in one of the corners of the vast room. Some other patients were walking nearby and Veronika tried to join them in order to eavesdrop on what the group members were saying.

She tried to disguise her intentions as best she could, but whenever she came close, they all fell silent and turned as one to look at her.

'What do you want?' said an elderly man, who seemed to be the leader of the Fraternity (if such a group really existed, and Zedka was not actually madder than she seemed).

'Nothing, I was just passing.'

They exchanged glances, and made a few mad gestures with their heads. One said to the other: 'She was just passing.' The other repeated the remark more loudly this time and soon they were all shouting the same words.

Veronika didn't know what to do and stood there paralysed with fear. A burly, shifty-looking male nurse came over, wanting to know what was going on.

'Nothing,' said one member of the group. 'She was just passing. She's standing right there, but she's still just passing.'

The whole group fell about laughing. Veronika assumed an ironic air, smiled, turned and moved off, so that no one would notice that her eyes were filling with tears. She went straight out into the garden, without bothering to put on a coat or jacket. A nurse tried to convince her to come back in, but another appeared soon after and whispered something in his ear, and the two of them left her in peace, in the cold. There was no point taking care of the health of someone who was condemned to die.

She was confused, tense, irritated with herself. She had never allowed herself to be provoked; she had learned from early on that, whenever a new situation presented itself, you had to remain cool and distant. Those mad people, however, had managed to make her feel shame, fear, rage, a desire to murder them all, to wound them with words she hadn't dared to utter.

Perhaps the pills or the treatment they had administered to get her out of her coma had transformed her into a frail woman, incapable of fending for herself. She had confronted far worse situations in her adolescence, and yet for the first time, she had been unable to hold back her tears. She needed to get back to the person she used to be, someone able to respond with irony, to pretend that the insults didn't bother her because she was better than all of them. Who, in that group, had had the courage to desire death? Who amongst them could teach her about life when they were all huddled behind the walls of Villete? She would never want to depend on their help for anything, even if she had to wait five or six days to die.

'One day's already gone. There are only another four or five left.'

She walked a little, letting the freezing cold enter her body and calm the blood that was flowing too fast, her heart that was beating too hard.

'Honestly, here I am, with my days literally numbered, giving importance to remarks made by people I've never even seen before, people who soon I'll never see again. And yet I suffer and get upset, I want to attack and defend. Why waste my time?'

38

But she *was* wasting the little time left to her, fighting for her tiny bit of space in that strange community where you had to put up a fight if you didn't want others imposing their rules on you.

'I can't believe it, I never used to be like this. I never used to fight over stupid things.'

She stopped in the middle of the icy garden. It was precisely because she had found everything so stupid that she had ended up accepting what life had naturally imposed on her. In adolescence, she thought it was too early to choose; now, in youth, she was convinced it was too late to change.

And what had she spent all her energies on until then? On trying to ensure that her life continued exactly as it always had. She had given up many of her desires so that her parents would continue to love her as they had when she was a child, even though she knew that real love changes and grows with time and discovers new ways of expressing itself. One day, when she had listened to her mother telling her, in tears, that her marriage was over, Veronika had sought out her father; she had cried, threatened and finally extracted a promise from him that he would not leave home, never imagining the high price her parents would have to pay for this.

When she decided to get a job, she rejected a tempting offer from a company that had just been set up in her recently created country in favour of a job at the public library, where you didn't earn much money, but where you were secure. She went to work every day, always keeping to the same timetable, always making sure she wasn't perceived as a threat by her superiors; she was contented, she didn't struggle and so she didn't grow: all she wanted was her salary at the end of the month.

She rented the room in the convent because the nuns required all tenants to be back at a certain hour, and then they locked the door: anyone still outside after that had to sleep in

39

the street. She always had a genuine excuse to give boyfriends, so as not to have to spend the night in hotel rooms or strange beds.

When she used to dream of getting married, she imagined herself in a little house outside Ljubljana, with a man quite different from her father, a man who earned enough to support his family, one who would be contented just to be with her in a house with an open fire and to look out at the snow-covered mountains.

She had taught herself to give men a precise amount of pleasure, never more, never less, only what was necessary. She didn't get angry with anyone, because that would mean having to react, having to do battle with the enemy, and then having to face unforeseen consequences, such as vengeance.

When she had achieved almost everything she wanted in life, she had reached the conclusion that her existence had no meaning, because every day was the same. And she had decided to die.

Veronika went back in and walked over to the group gathered in one corner of the room. The people were talking animatedly, but fell silent as soon as she approached.

She went straight over to the oldest man, who seemed to be the leader. Before anyone could stop her, she gave him a resounding slap in the face.

'Aren't you going to react?' she asked out loud, so that everyone in the room could hear her. 'Aren't you going to do something?'

'No,' the man said and passed a hand over his face. A little thread of blood ran from his nose. 'You won't be troubling us for very long.'

She left the lounge and went triumphantly back to her ward. She had done something that she had never done in her entire life.

Three days had passed since the incident with the group that Zedka called the Fraternity. Veronika regretted that slap, not because she was afraid of the man's reaction, but because she had done something different. If she wasn't careful, she might end up convinced that life was worth living, and that would cause her pointless pain, since she would soon have to leave this world anyway.

Her only option was to keep away from everything and everyone, to try to be in every way as she had been before, to obey Villete's rules and regulations. She adapted herself to the routine imposed by the hospital: rising early, having breakfast, going for a walk in the garden, having lunch, going to the lounge, for another walk in the garden, then supper, television and bed.

Before Veronika went to sleep, a nurse always appeared with medication. All the other women took pills, Veronika was the only one who was given an injection. She never complained, she just wanted to know why she was given so many sedatives, since she had never had any problems sleeping. They explained that the injection was not a sedative, but medication for her heart.

And so, by falling in with that routine, her days in the hospital all began to seem the same. When the days are all the same, they pass more quickly; in another two or three days she would no longer have to brush her teeth or comb her hair. Veronika noticed her heart growing rapidly weaker: she became easily out of breath, she got pains in her chest, she had no appetite, and the slightest effort made her dizzy.

After the incident with the Fraternity, she had sometimes thought: 'If I had a choice, if I had understood earlier that the reason my days were all the same was because I wanted them like that, perhaps...'

But the reply was always the same: 'There is no perhaps, because there is no choice.' And her inner peace returned, because everything had already been decided.

During this period, she formed a relationship with Zedka (not a friendship, because friendship requires a lot of time spent together, and that wouldn't be possible). They used to play cards – which helps the time pass more rapidly – and sometimes they would walk together, in silence, in the garden.

On one particular morning, immediately after breakfast, they all went out to take the sun, as the regulations demanded. A nurse, however, asked Zedka to go back to the ward, because it was her treatment day.

Veronika, who was having breakfast with her, heard the request.

'What treatment's that?'

'It's an old treatment, from the sixties, but the doctors think it might hasten my recovery. Do you want to come and watch?'

'You said you were depressed. Isn't taking the medication enough to replace the chemical you're lacking?'

'Do you want to watch?' insisted Zedka.

She was going to step outside the routine, thought Veronika. She was going to discover new things, when she didn't need to learn anything more – all she needed was patience. But her curiosity got the better of her and she nodded.

'This isn't a show, you know,' said the nurse.

'She's going to die. She's hardly seen anything. Let her come with us.'

Veronika watched the woman, still smiling, being strapped to the bed.

'Tell her what's going on,' said Zedka to the male nurse. 'Otherwise she'll be frightened.'

He turned and showed her the syringe. He seemed pleased to be treated like a doctor, explaining to a younger doctor the correct procedures and the proper treatments.

'This syringe contains a dose of insulin,' he said, speaking in a grave, technical tone of voice. 'It's used by diabetics to combat high blood glucose. However, when the dose is much larger than normal, the consequent drop in blood glucose provokes a state of coma.'

He tapped the needle lightly, to get rid of any air, and then stuck it in a vein in Zedka's right foot.

'That's what's going to happen now. She's going to enter a state of induced coma. Don't be frightened if her eyes go glazed, and don't expect her to recognise you when she's under the effects of the medication.'

'That's awful, inhuman. People struggle to get out of a coma not to go into one.'

'People struggle to live, not to commit suicide,' replied the nurse, but Veronika ignored the remark. 'And a state of coma allows the organism to rest; its functions are all drastically reduced and any existing tension disappears.'

While he was talking, he was injecting the liquid, and Zedka's eyes were growing dull.

'Don't worry,' Veronika was saying to her. 'You're absolutely normal, the story you told me about the king...'

'Don't waste your time. She can't hear you any more.'

The woman on the bed, who a few minutes before had seemed so lucid and full of life, now had her eyes fixed on some point in the distance, and there was liquid bubbling from one corner of her mouth.

'What did you do?' she shouted at the nurse.

'Just my job.'

Veronika started calling to Zedka, shouting, threatening that she would go to the police, the press, the human rights organisations.

'Calm down. You may be in a mental hospital, but you still have to abide by certain rules.'

She saw that the man was utterly serious and she was afraid. But since she had nothing to lose, she went on shouting.

From where she was, Zedka could see the ward and the beds, all empty except for one, to which her body was strapped, and beside which a girl was standing, staring in horror. The girl didn't know that the person in the bed was still alive with all her biological functions working perfectly, but that her soul was flying, almost touching the ceiling, experiencing a sense of profound peace.

Zedka was making an astral journey, something that had been a surprise during her first experience of insulin shock. She hadn't mentioned it to anyone, she was only there to be cured of depression and, as soon as she was in a fit state, she hoped to leave that place for ever. If she started telling them that she had left her body, they would think she was madder than when she had entered Villete. However, as soon as she had returned to her body, she began reading up on both subjects: insulin shock and that strange feeling of floating in space.

There wasn't much written about the treatment. It had been used for the first time around 1930, but had been completely banned in psychiatric hospitals, because of the possibility of irreversible damage to the patient. During one such session, she had visited Dr Igor's office in her astral form, at precisely the moment when he was discussing the subject with one of the owners of the hospital. 'It's a crime,' Dr Igor was saying. 'Yes, but it's cheap and it's quick!' replied the other man. 'Anyway,

45

who's interested in the rights of the mad? No one's going to complain.'

Even so, some doctors still considered it a quick way of treating depression. Zedka had sought out and borrowed everything that had been written about insulin shock, especially first-hand reports by patients who had experienced it. The story was always the same: horrors and more horrors, not one of them had experienced anything resembling what she was living through at that moment.

She concluded – quite rightly – that there was no relationship between insulin and the feeling that her consciousness was leaving her body. On the contrary, the tendency with that kind of treatment was to diminish the patient's mental capacity.

She started researching into the existence of the soul, read a few books on occultism, and then, one day, she stumbled on a vast literature that described exactly what she was experiencing: it was called 'astral travel' and many people had already had the same experience. Some had merely set out to describe what they had felt, while others had developed techniques to provoke it. Zedka now knew those techniques by heart and she used them every night to go wherever she wished.

The descriptions of those experiences and visions varied, but they all had certain points in common: the strange, irritating noise that preceded the separation of the body from the spirit, followed by a shock, a rapid loss of consciousness, and then the peace and joy of floating in the air, attached to the body by a silvery cord, a cord that could be stretched indefinitely, although there were legends (in books, of course) that said the person would die if they allowed that silver thread to break.

Her experience, however, showed that she could go as far as she wanted and the cord never broke. But, generally speaking, the books had been very useful in teaching her how to get more and more out of her astral travelling. She had learned, for example, that when she wanted to move from one place to another, she had to concentrate on projecting herself into space, imagining where exactly she wanted to go. Unlike the routes followed by planes – which leave from one place and fly the necessary distance to reach another – an astral journey was made through mysterious tunnels. You imagined yourself in a place, you entered the appropriate tunnel at a terrifying speed, and the other place would appear.

It was through books too that she had lost her fear of the creatures inhabiting space. Today there was no one else in the ward, but the first time she had left her body, she had found a lot of people watching her, amused by her look of surprise.

Her first reaction was to assume that these were dead people, ghosts haunting the hospital. Then, with the help of books and of her own experience, she realised that, although there were a few disembodied spirits wandering about there, amongst them were people as alive as she was, who had either developed the technique of leaving their bodies, or who were not even aware of what was happening to them because, in some other part of the world, they were sleeping deeply, while their spirits roamed freely abroad.

Today – knowing that this was her last astral journey on insulin, because she had just been to visit Dr Igor's office and overheard him saying he was ready to release her – she decided to remain inside Villete. From the moment she went out through the main gate, she would never again return, not even in spirit, and she wanted to say goodbye.

To say goodbye. That was the really difficult part: once in a mental hospital, a person grows used to the freedom that exists in the world of madness and becomes addicted to it. You no longer have to take on responsibilities, to struggle to earn your daily bread, to be bothered with repetitive, mundane tasks. You could spend hours looking at a picture or making absurd doodles. Everything is tolerated because, after all, the person is mentally ill. As she herself had had occasion to observe, most of the inmates showed a marked improvement once they entered the hospital: they no longer had to hide their symptoms, and the 'family' atmosphere helped them to accept their own neuroses and psychoses.

At the beginning, Zedka had been fascinated by Villete and had even considered joining the Fraternity once she was cured. But she realised that if she was sensible, she could continue doing everything she enjoyed doing outside, as long as she dealt with the challenges of daily life. As someone had said, all you had to do was to keep your madness under control. You could cry, get worried or angry like any other normal human being, as long as you remembered that, up above, your spirit was laughing out loud at all those thorny situations.

She would soon be back home, with her children and her husband, and that part of her life also had its charms. Of course it would be difficult to find work; after all, in a small town like Ljubljana news travels fast, and her internment in Villete was already common knowledge to many people. But her husband earned enough to keep the family, and she could use her free time to continue making her astral journeys, though not under the dangerous influence of insulin.

There was only one thing she did not want to experience again, the reason that had brought her to Villete.

Depression.

The doctors said that a recently discovered substance, serotonin, was one of the compounds responsible for how human beings felt. A lack of serotonin impaired one's capacity to concentrate at work, to sleep, to eat and to enjoy life's pleasures. When this substance was completely absent, the person experienced despair, pessimism, a sense of futility, terrible tiredness, anxiety, difficulties in making decisions, and would end up sinking into permanent gloom, which would lead either to complete apathy or to suicide.

Other more conservative doctors said that any drastic change in life could trigger depression – moving to another country, losing a loved one, divorce, an increase in the demands of work or family. Some modern studies, based on the number of internments in winter and summer, pointed to the lack of sunlight as one of the causes of depression.

In Zedka's case, however, the reasons were simpler than anyone suspected: a man hidden in her past, or rather, the fantasy she had built up about a man she had known a long time ago.

It was so stupid. Plunging into depression and madness all because of a man whose current whereabouts she didn't even know, but with whom she had fallen hopelessly in love in her youth, since, like every normal young girl, Zedka had needed to experience the Impossible Love.

However, unlike her friends, who only dreamed of the Impossible Love, Zedka had decided to go further; she had actually tried to realise that dream. He lived on the other side of the ocean and she sold up everything to go and join him. He was married, but she accepted her role as mistress, plotting secretly to make him her husband. He barely had enough time for himself, but she resigned herself to spending days and nights in a cheap hotel room, waiting for his rare telephone calls.

Despite her determination to put up with everything in the name of love, the relationship did not work out. He never said anything directly, but one day, Zedka realised that she was no longer welcome and she returned to Slovenia.

She spent a few months barely eating and remembering every second they had spent together, reviewing again and again their moments of joy and pleasure in bed, trying to fix on something that would allow her to believe in the future of that relationship. Her friends were worried about the state she was in, but something in Zedka's heart told her it was just a passing phase; personal growth has its price, and she was paying it without complaint. And so it was: one morning she woke up with an immense will to live; for the first time in ages, she ate heartily and then went out and found a job. She found not only a job, but also the attentions of a handsome, intelligent young man, much sought after by other women. A year later, she was married to him.

She aroused both the envy and the applause of her girl-friends. The two of them went to live in a comfortable house, with a garden that looked over the river that flows through Ljubljana. They had children and took trips to Austria or Italy during the summer.

When Slovenia decided to separate from Yugoslavia, he was called up into the army. Zedka was a Serb – that is, the enemy – and her life seemed on the point of collapse. In the ten tense days that followed, with the troops prepared for confrontation, and no one knowing quite what the result of the declaration of independence would be and how much blood would have to be spilt because of it, Zedka realised how much she loved him. She spent the whole time praying to a God who, until then, had seemed remote, but who now seemed her only hope. She promised the saints and angels anything as long as she could have her husband back.

And so it was. He came back, the children were able to go to schools where they taught the Slovene language, and the threat of war shifted to the neighbouring republic of Croatia.

Three years had passed. Yugoslavia's war with Croatia moved to Bosnia, and reports began to circulate of massacres committed by the Serbs. Zedka thought it unjust to label a whole nation as criminals because of the folly of a few madmen. Her life took on a meaning she had never expected: she defended her people with pride and courage, writing in newspapers, appearing on television, organising conferences. None of this bore any fruit, and even today, foreigners still believe all the Serbs were responsible for those atrocities, but Zedka knew she had done her duty, and that she could not abandon her brothers and sisters at such a difficult time. She could count on the support of her Slovene husband, of her children, and of people who were not manipulated by the propaganda machines of either side.

One evening, she walked past the statue of Prešeren, the great Slovene poet, and she began to think about his life. When he was thirty-four, he went into a church and saw an adolescent girl, Julia Primic, with whom he fell passionately in love. Like the ancient minstrels, he began to write her poems, in the hope of one day marrying her.

It turned out that Julia was the daughter of an upper middle-class family and, apart from that chance sighting inside the church, Prešeren never again managed to get near her. But that encounter inspired his finest poetry and created a whole legend around his name. In the small central square of Ljubljana, the statue of the poet stares fixedly at something. If you follow his gaze, you will see, on the other side of the square, the face of a woman carved into the stone of one of the houses. That was where Julia had lived. Even after death, Prešeren gazes for all eternity on his Impossible Love.

And what if he had fought a little harder?

Zedka's heart started beating fast, perhaps it was a presentiment of something bad, an accident involving one of her children. She raced back home only to find them watching television and eating popcorn.

That sadness, however, did not pass. Zedka lay down and slept for nearly twelve hours and, when she woke, she didn't feel like getting up. Prešeren's story had brought back to her the image of her first lover, who had never again contacted her.

And Zedka asked herself: did I fight hard enough? Should I have accepted my role as mistress, rather than wanting things to go as I expected them to? Did I fight for my first love with the same energy with which I fought for my people?

Zedka persuaded herself that she had, but the sadness would not go away. What once had seemed to her a Paradise – the house near the river, the husband whom she loved, the children eating popcorn in front of the television – was gradually transformed into a hell.

Today, after many astral journeys and many encounters with highly evolved beings, Zedka knew that this was all nonsense. She had used her Impossible Love as an excuse, a pretext for breaking the ties with the life she led, and which was far from being the life she really expected for herself.

But twelve months earlier, the situation had been quite different: she began frantically looking for that distant lover, she spent a fortune on international phone calls, but he no longer lived in the same city, and it was impossible to find him. She sent letters by express mail, which were always returned. She phoned all his friends, but no one had any idea what had happened to him.

Her husband was completely unaware of what was going on, and that infuriated her, because he should at least have suspected something, made a scene, complained, threatened to put her out in the street. She became convinced that the international telephone operators, the postman and all her girlfriends had been bribed by him to pretend indifference. She sold the jewellery that had been given to her when she married and bought a plane ticket to the other side of the ocean, until someone managed to convince her that America was a very large place and there was no point going there if you didn't know quite what you were looking for.

One evening, she lay down, suffering for love as she had never suffered before, not even when she had come back to the awful day-to-day life of Ljubljana. She spent that night and the following two days in her room. On the third day, her husband – so kind, so concerned about her – called a doctor. Did he really not know that Zedka was trying to get in touch with the other man, to commit adultery, to exchange her life as a respected wife for life as someone's secret mistress, to leave Ljubljana, her home, her children for ever?

The doctor arrived. She became hysterical and locked the door, and only opened it again when the doctor had left. A week later, she no longer had sufficient strength of will to get out of bed and began to use the bed as a toilet. She did not think any more, her head was completely taken up by fragmentary memories of the man who, she was convinced, was also unsuccessfully looking for her.

Her infuriatingly generous husband changed the sheets, smoothed her hair, said that it would all be all right in the end. The children no longer came into her bedroom, ever since she had slapped one of them for no reason, and then knelt down, kissed his feet, begging forgiveness, tearing her nightdress into shreds in order to show her despair and repentance.

After another week, in which she spat out the food offered to her, drifted in and out of reality several times, spent whole nights awake and whole days asleep, two men came into her room without knocking. One of them held her down while the other gave her an injection, and she woke up in Villete.

'Depression,' she heard the doctor say to her husband. 'Sometimes it's provoked by the most banal things, for example, the lack of a chemical substance, serotonin, in the organism.'

From the ceiling in the ward, Zedka watched the nurse approaching, syringe in hand. The girl was still standing there, trying to talk to her body, terrified by her vacant gaze. For some moments, Zedka considered the possibility of telling her about everything that was happening, but then she changed her mind; people never learn anything by being told, they have to find out for themselves.

The nurse placed the needle in Zedka's arm and injected her with glucose. As if grabbed by an enormous arm, her spirit left the ceiling, sped through a dark tunnel and returned to her body.

'Hello, Veronika.'

The girl looked frightened.

'Are you all right?'

'Yes, I'm fine. Fortunately, I've managed to survive this dangerous treatment, but it won't be repeated.'

'How do you know? Here no one respects the patient's wishes.'

Zedka knew because, during her astral journey, she had gone to Dr Igor's office.

'I can't explain why, I just know. Do you remember the first question I ever asked you?'

'Yes, you asked me if I knew what being mad meant?'

'Exactly. This time I'm not going to tell you a story.

Madness is the inability to communicate your ideas. It's as if you were in a foreign country, able to see and understand everything that's going on around you, but incapable of explaining what you need to know or of being helped, because you don't understand the language they speak there.'

'We've all felt that.'

'And all of us, one way or another, are mad.'

Outside the barred window, the sky was thick with stars, and the moon, in its first quarter, was rising behind the mountains. Poets loved the full moon, they wrote thousands of poems about it, but it was the new moon that Veronika loved best because there was still room for it to grow, to expand, to fill the whole of its surface with light before its inevitable decline.

She felt like going over to the piano in the lounge, and celebrating that night with a lovely sonata she had learned at school. Looking up at the sky, she had an indescribable sense of well-being, as if the infinite nature of the universe had revealed her own eternity to her. However, she was separated from her desire by a steel door and a woman who was always endlessly reading a book. Besides, no one played the piano at that hour of night, she would wake up the whole neighbourhood.

Veronika laughed. The 'neighbourhood' were the wards full of mad people, and those mad people were, in turn, full of drugs to make them sleep.

Her sense of well-being continued though. She got up and went over to Zedka's bed, but she was sound asleep too, perhaps recovering from the horrible experience she had been through.

'Go back to bed,' said the nurse. 'Good girls should be dreaming of angels or lovers.'

'Don't treat me like a child. I'm not some tame mad woman who's afraid of everything, I'm raving, hysterical, I don't even respect my own life, or the lives of others. Anyway, today I'm in a bad way. I've looked at the moon and I need to talk to someone.'

The nurse looked at her, surprised by her reaction.

'Are you afraid of me?' asked Veronika. 'In a couple of days' time I'll be dead, what have I got to lose?'

'Why don't you go for a walk, dear, and let me finish my book?'

'Because this is a prison and there's a prison warder pretending to read a book, just to make others think she's an intelligent woman. The fact is, though, that she's watching every movement in the ward, and she guards the keys to the door as if they were a treasure. It's doubtless all in the regulations and so she must obey, because that way she can pretend to an authority she doesn't have in her everyday life, with her husband and children.'

Veronika was trembling, without quite knowing why.

'Keys?' said the nurse. 'The door is always open. You don't think I'd stay locked up in here with a load of mental patients, do you?'

What does she mean the door's open? A few days ago I wanted to get out of here, and this woman even went with me to the toilet. What is she talking about?

'Don't take me too seriously,' said the nurse. 'The fact is we don't need a lot of security here, because of the sedatives we dole out. You're shivering, are you cold?'

'I don't know. I think it must be something to do with my heart.'

'If you like, you can go for a walk.'

'What I'd really like is to play the piano.'

'The lounge is quite separate, so your piano playing won't disturb anyone. Do what you like.'

Veronika's trembling changed into low, timid, suppressed sobs. She knelt down, lay her head on the woman's lap and cried and cried.

The nurse put down the book, and stroked Veronika's hair, allowing that wave of sadness and tears its natural expression. There they sat, for almost half an hour, one crying, the other consoling, though neither knew why or what.

The sobbing finally ceased. The nurse helped her up, took her by the arm and led her to the door.

'I've got a daughter your age. When you were first admitted, full of drips and tubes, I kept wondering why a pretty young girl, with her whole life ahead of her, should want to kill herself. Then all kinds of rumours started flying around: about the letter that you left behind, which I never believed could be the real motive, and how you didn't have long to live because of some incurable heart problem. I couldn't get the image of my own daughter out of my head: what if she decided to do something like that? Why do certain people try to go against the natural order of things, which is to fight for survival whatever happens?'

'That's why I was crying,' said Veronika. 'When I took the pills, I wanted to kill someone I hated. I didn't know that other Veronikas existed inside me, Veronikas that I could love.'

'What makes a person hate themselves?'

'Cowardice perhaps. Or the eternal fear of being wrong, of not doing what others expect. A few moments ago I was happy, I forgot I was under sentence of death; then, when I remembered the situation I'm in, I felt frightened.'

The nurse opened the door and Veronika went out.

How could she ask me that? What does she want, to understand why I was crying? Doesn't she realise I'm a perfectly normal person, with the same desires and fears as everyone else, and that a question like that, now that it's all too late, could throw me into panic?

As she was walking down the corridors, lit by the same faint light as in the ward, Veronika realised that it *was* too late: she could no longer control her fear.

'I must get a grip on myself. I'm the kind of person who sticks to any decision she makes, who always sees things through.'

It's true that in her life she had seen many things through to their ultimate consequences, but only unimportant things, like prolonging a quarrel that could easily have been resolved with an apology, or not phoning a man she was in love with, simply because she thought the relationship would lead nowhere. She was intransigent about the easy things, as if trying to prove to herself how strong and indifferent she was, when, in fact, she was just a fragile woman, who had never been an outstanding student, never excelled at school sports and had never succeeded in keeping the peace at home.

She had overcome her minor defects, only to be defeated by matters of fundamental importance. She had managed to appear utterly independent, when she was, in fact, desperately in need of company. When she entered a room, everyone would turn to look at her, but she almost always ended the night alone, in the convent, watching a TV that she hadn't even bothered to have properly tuned in. She gave all her friends the impression that she was a woman to be envied, and she expended most of her energy in trying to behave in accordance with the image she had created of herself.

Because of that, she had never had enough energy to be herself, a person who, like everyone else in the world, needed other people in order to be happy. But other people were so difficult.

They reacted in unpredictable ways, they surrounded themselves with defensive walls, they behaved just as she did, pretending they didn't care about anything. When someone more open to life appeared, they either rejected them outright, or made them suffer, considering them inferior, 'ingenuous'.

She may have impressed a lot of people with her strength and determination, but where had it left her? In the void. Utterly alone. In Villete. In the anteroom of death.

Veronika's remorse over her attempted suicide resurfaced, and she firmly pushed it away again. Now she was feeling something she had never allowed herself to feel: hatred.

Hatred. Something almost as physical as walls, pianos or nurses; she could almost touch the destructive energy leaking out of her body. She allowed the feeling to emerge, regardless of whether it was good or bad, she was sick of self-control, of masks, of appropriate behaviour. Veronika wanted to spend her remaining two or three days of life behaving as inappropriately as she could.

She had begun by slapping an old man in the face, she had burst into tears in front of a nurse, she had refused to be nice and to talk to the others when what she really wanted was to be alone, and now she was free enough to feel hatred, although intelligent enough not to smash everything around her and risk spending what remained of her life under sedation and in a bed in a ward.

At that moment, she hated everything: herself, the world, the chair in front of her, the broken radiator in one of the corridors, people who were perfect, criminals. She was in a mental hospital and so could allow herself to feel things that people usually hide from themselves, because we are all brought up only to love, to accept, to look for ways round things, to avoid conflict. Veronika hated everything, but mainly she hated the way she had lived her life, never bothering to discover the hundreds of other Veronikas who lived inside her and who were interesting, mad, curious, brave, bold.

Then she started to feel hatred for the person she loved most in the world: her mother. A wonderful wife who worked all day and washed the dishes at night, sacrificing her own life so that her daughter would have a good education, know how to play the piano and the violin, dress like a princess, have the latest trainers and jeans, while she mended the same old dress she had worn for years.

'How can I hate someone who only ever gave me love?' thought Veronika, confused, trying to check her feelings. But it was too late, her hatred had been unleashed, she had opened the door to her personal hell. She hated the love she had been given, because it had asked for nothing in return, which was absurd, unreal, against the laws of nature.

That love asking for nothing in return had managed to fill her with guilt, with a desire to fulfil another's expectations, even if that meant giving up everything she had dreamed of for herself. It was a love that for years had tried to hide from her the difficulties and the corruption that existed in the world, ignoring the fact that, one day, she would have to find this out, and would then be defenceless against them.

And her father? She hated her father too, because, unlike her mother, who worked all the time, he knew how to live, he took her to bars and to the theatre, they had fun together, and when he was still young, she had loved him secretly, not the way one loves a father, but as a man. She hated him because he had always been so charming and so open with everyone except her mother, the only person who really deserved such treatment.

She hated everything. The library with its pile of books full of explanations about life, the school that had forced her to spend whole evenings learning algebra, even though she didn't know a single person, apart from teachers and mathematicians, who needed algebra in order to be happy. Why did they make them learn so much algebra or geometry or any of that mountain of other useless things?

Veronika pushed open the door to the lounge, went over to the piano, opened the lid, and, summoning up all her strength, pounded on the keys. A mad, cacophonous, jangled chord echoed round the empty room, bounced off the walls and returned to her in the guise of a shrill sound that seemed to tear at her soul. Yet it was an accurate portrait of her soul at that moment.

She pounded on the keys again, and again the dissonant notes reverberated about her.

'I'm mad. I'm allowed to do this. I can hate, I can pound away at the piano. Since when have mental patients known how to play notes in the right order?'

She pounded the piano again, once, twice, ten, twenty times, and each time she did it, her hatred seemed to diminish, until it passed away completely.

Then, once more, a deep peace flooded through her and Veronika again looked out at the starry sky and at the new moon, her favourite, filling the room she was in with gentle light. The impression returned of Infinity and Eternity walking hand in hand; you only had to look for one of them, for example, the limitless universe, to feel the presence of the other, Time that never ends, that never passes, that remains in the Present, where all of life's secrets lie. As she had been walking from the ward to that room, she had felt such pure hatred that now she had no more rancour left in her heart. She had finally allowed her negative feelings to surface, feelings that had been repressed

for years in her soul. She had actually *felt* them, and they were
no longer necessary, they could leave.

She sat on in silence, enjoying the present moment, letting love
fill up the empty space left behind by hatred. When she felt the
moment had come, she turned to the moon and played a sonata
in homage to it, knowing that the moon was listening and
would feel proud, and that this would provoke the jealousy of
the stars. Then she played music for the stars, for the garden,
for the mountains that she could not see in the darkness, but
which she knew were there.

While she was playing that music for the garden, another
mad person appeared, Eduard, a schizophrenic who was beyond
all cure. She was not frightened by his presence; on the contrary,
she smiled, and to her surprise, he smiled back.

The music could even penetrate his remote world, more distant than the moon itself; it could even perform miracles.

'I must buy a new key ring,' thought Dr Igor, as he opened the door to his small consulting room in Villete. The old one was falling to pieces and a small decorative metal shield had just fallen to the floor.

Dr Igor bent down and picked it up. What should he do with that shield bearing the Ljubljana coat of arms? He might as well throw it away, although he could have it mended and ask them to make a new leather strap, or else he could give it to his nephew to play with. Both alternatives seemed equally absurd. A key ring doesn't cost very much and his nephew had no interest in shields; he spent all his time watching television, or playing with electronic toys imported from Italy. Dr Igor could still not bring himself to throw it out, however, so he put it back in his pocket; he would decide what to do with it later on.

That was why he was the director of the hospital and not a patient, because he thought a lot before making any decisions.

He turned on the light; as winter advanced, dawn came ever later. Moving house, getting divorced and the absence of light were the main reasons for the increase in the number of cases of depression. Dr Igor was hoping that spring would arrive early and solve half his problems.

He looked at his diary for the day. He needed to find some way to prevent Eduard from dying of hunger; his schizophrenia made him unpredictable, and now he had stopped eating. Dr

Igor had already prescribed intravenous feeding, but he could-n't keep that up for ever. Eduard was a strong young man of twenty-eight, but even with a drip, he would eventually waste away, becoming more and more skeletal.

What would Eduard's father think? He was one of the young Slovene republic's best-known ambassadors. He had been one of the people behind the delicate negotiations with Yugoslavia in the early 1990s. He, after all, had managed to work for years for the Belgrade government, surviving his detractors, who accused him of working for the enemy, and he was still in the diplomatic corps, except, this time, he represent-ed a different country. He was a powerful and influential man, feared by everyone.

Dr Igor felt momentarily worried, just as before he had been worried about the shield on his key ring, but he immedi-ately dismissed the thought. As far as the ambassador was con-cerned, it didn't matter whether his son looked well or not; he had no intention of taking him to official functions or having him accompany him to the various places in the world where he was sent as a government representative. Eduard was in Villete, and there he would stay for ever, or at least as long as his father continued earning his nice, fat salary.

Dr Igor decided to stop the intravenous feeding, and allow Eduard to waste away a little more, until he himself felt like eating. If the situation got worse, he would write a report and pass responsibility on to the council of doctors who adminis-tered Villete. 'The best way to avoid trouble is to share respon-sibility,' his father had taught him. He had been a doctor too, and although he had had various deaths on his hands, he had never had any problem with the authorities.

Once Dr Igor had ordered Eduard's treatment to stop, he moved on to the next case. According to the report, Zedka Mendel had completed her course of treatment and could be allowed to leave. Dr Igor wanted to see for himself. There was nothing a doctor dreaded more than getting complaints from the families of patients who had been in Villete, which was what nearly always happened, for it was rare for a patient to readjust successfully to normal life after a period spent in a mental hospital.

It wasn't the fault of the hospital, nor of any of the hospitals scattered round the world; the problem of readjustment was exactly the same everywhere. Just as prison never corrects the prisoner – it only teaches him to commit more crimes – so hospitals merely got patients used to a completely unreal world, where everything was allowed and where no one had to take responsibility for their actions.

There was only one way out: to discover a cure for insanity. And Dr Igor was engaged heart and soul on just that, developing a thesis that would revolutionise the psychiatric world. In mental hospitals, temporary patients who lived alongside incurable patients began a process of social degeneration which, once started, was impossible to stop. Zedka Mendel would come back to hospital eventually, this time of her own volition, complaining of non-existent ailments, simply in order to be close to people who seemed to understand her better than those in the outside world.

If, however, he could find a way of combating Vitriol, the poison which Dr Igor believed to be the cause of madness, his name would go down in history and people would finally know where Slovenia was. That week, he had been given a heaven-sent opportunity in the shape of a would-be suicide; he was not going to lose this opportunity for all the money in the world.

Dr Igor felt happy. Although he was obliged for economic reasons to accept treatments, like insulin shock for example, that had long ago been condemned by the medical profession, the same economic reasons lay behind Villete's instigation of a new psychiatric treatment. As well as having the time and the staff to carry out his researches into Vitriol, he also had the owners' permission to allow the group calling itself the Fraternity to remain in the hospital. The shareholders in the institution tolerated – note that word well, not encouraged, but tolerated – a longer period of internment than was strictly necessary. They argued that, for humanitarian reasons, they should give the recently-cured the option of deciding for themselves when would be the best moment for them to rejoin the world, and that had led to a group of people deciding to stay in Villete, as if at a select hotel, or a club for those with similar interests and views. Thus Dr Igor managed to keep the mad and the sane in the same place, allowing the latter to have a positive influence on the former. To prevent things from degenerating and to stop the mad having a negative effect on those who had been cured, every member of the Fraternity had to leave the hospital at least once a day.

Dr Igor knew that the reasons given by the shareholders for allowing the presence of healthy people in the hospital – 'humanitarian reasons' they said – were just an excuse. They were afraid that Ljubljana, Slovenia's small but charming capital, did not have a sufficient number of wealthy mad people to sustain this expensive, modern building. Besides, the public health system ran a number of first-class mental hospitals of its own, and that left Villete at a disadvantage in the mental health market.

When the shareholders had converted the old barracks into a hospital, their target market had been the men and women likely to be affected by the war with Yugoslavia. The war, however, had been brief. The shareholders had felt certain that war would return, but it didn't.

Moreover, recent research had shown that whilst wars did have their psychological victims, they were far fewer than, say, the victims of stress, tedium, congenital illness, loneliness and rejection. When a community had a major problem to face, for example, war, hyperinflation or plague, there was a slight increase in the number of suicides, but a marked decline in cases of depression, paranoia and psychosis. These returned to their normal levels as soon as that problem had been overcome, indicating, or so Dr Igor thought, that people only allow themselves the luxury of being mad when they are in a position to do so.

He had before him another recent survey, this time from Canada, which an American newspaper had recently voted the country with the highest standard of living. Dr Igor read:

According to *Statistics Canada*, 40% of people between 15 and 34, 33% of people between 35 and 54 and 20% of people between 55 and 64 have already had some kind of mental illness. It is thought that one in every five individuals suffers some form of psychiatric disorder and one in every eight Canadians will be hospitalised at least once in their lifetime because of mental disturbances.

'They've got a bigger market there than we have,' he thought. 'The happier people can be, the unhappier they are.'

Dr Igor analysed a few more cases, thinking carefully about those he should share with the council and those he should resolve alone. By the time he had finished, day had broken, and he turned off the light.

He immediately ordered his first appointment to be shown in: the mother of the patient who had tried to commit suicide.

'I'm Veronika's mother. How is my daughter?'

Dr Igor wondered if he should tell her the truth and save her any unpleasant surprises – after all, he had a daughter with the same name – but he decided it was best to say nothing.

'We don't yet know,' he lied. 'We need another week.'

'I've no idea why Veronika did it,' said the woman tearfully. 'We've always been loving parents, we sacrificed everything to give her the best possible upbringing. Although my husband and I have had our ups and downs, we've kept the family together, as an example of perseverance in adversity. She's got a good job, she's nice-looking, and yet...'

'... and yet she tried to kill herself,' said Dr Igor. 'There's no reason to be surprised, that's the way it is. People just can't cope with happiness. If you like, I could show you the statistics for Canada.'

'Canada?'

The woman seemed startled. Dr Igor saw that he had managed to distract her and went on.

'Look, you haven't come here to find out how your daughter is, but to apologise for the fact that she tried to commit suicide. How old is she?'

'Twenty-four.'

'So she's a mature, experienced woman who knows what she wants and is perfectly capable of making her own choices. What has that got to do with your marriage or with the sacrifices that you and your husband made? How long has she lived on her own?'

'Six years.'

'You see? She's fundamentally independent. But, because of what a certain Austrian doctor – Dr Sigmund Freud, I'm sure you've heard of him – wrote about unhealthy relationships between parents and children, people today still blame themselves for everything. Do you imagine that Indians believe that the son-turned-murderer is a victim of his parents' upbringing? Tell me.'

'I haven't the faintest idea,' replied the woman, who couldn't get over her bewilderment at the doctor's behaviour. Perhaps he was influenced by his patients.

'Well, I'll tell you,' said Dr Igor. 'The Indians believe the murderer to be guilty, not society, not his parents, not his ancestors. Do the Japanese commit suicide because a son of theirs decides to take drugs and go out and shoot people? The reply is the same: no! And, as we all know, the Japanese will commit suicide at the drop of a hat. The other day, I read that a young Japanese man killed himself because he had failed his university entrance exams.'

'Do you think I could talk to my daughter?' asked the woman, who was not interested in the Japanese, the Indians or the Canadians.

'Yes, yes, in a moment,' said Dr Igor, slightly annoyed by the interruption. 'But first, I want you to understand one thing: apart from certain grave pathological cases, people only go mad when they try to escape from routine. Do you understand?'

'I do,' she replied. 'And if you think that I won't be capable of looking after her, you can rest assured, I've *never* tried to change my life.'

'Good.' Dr Igor seemed relieved. 'Can you imagine a world in which, for example, we were not obliged to repeat the same thing every day of our lives? If, for example, we all decided to eat only when we were hungry, what would housewives and restaurants do?'

'It would be more normal to eat only when we were hungry,' thought the woman, but she said nothing, afraid that he might not let her speak to Veronika.

'Well, it would cause tremendous confusion,' she said at last. 'I'm a housewife myself, and I know what I'm talking about.'

'So we have breakfast, lunch and supper. We have to wake up at a certain hour every day and rest once a week. Christmas exists so that we can give each other presents, Easter so that we can spend a few days at the lake. How would you like it if your husband were gripped by a sudden, passionate impulse and decided he wanted to make love in the living room?'

The woman thought: 'What *is* the man talking about? I came here to see my daughter.'

'I would find it very sad,' she said, carefully, hoping she was giving the right answer.

'Excellent,' roared Dr Igor. 'The bedroom is the correct place for making love. To make love anywhere else would set a bad example and promote the spread of anarchy.'

'Can I see my daughter?' said the woman.

Dr Igor gave up. This peasant would never understand what he was talking about; she wasn't interested in discussing madness from a philosophical point of view, even though she knew her daughter had made a serious suicide attempt and had been in a coma.

He rang the bell and his secretary appeared.

'Call the young woman who tried to commit suicide,' he said. 'The one who wrote the letter to the newspapers, saying that she was killing herself in order to put Slovenia on the map.'

'I don't want to see her. I've cut all my links with the outside world.'

It had been hard to say that in the lounge, with everyone else there. But the nurse hadn't been exactly discreet either, and had announced in a loud voice that her mother was waiting to see her, as if it were a matter of general interest.

She didn't want to see her mother; it would only upset both of them. It was best that her mother should think of her as dead. Veronika had always hated goodbyes.

The man disappeared whence he had come, and she went back to looking at the mountains. After a week, the sun had finally returned, something she had known would happen the previous night, because the moon had told her while she was playing the piano.

'No, that's crazy, I'm losing my grip. Planets don't talk, or only to self-styled astrologers. If the moon spoke to anyone, it was to that schizophrenic.'

The very moment she thought this, she noticed a sharp pain in her chest, and her arm went numb. Veronika felt her head spinning. A heart attack!

She entered a kind of euphoric state, as if death had freed her from the fear of dying. So, it was all over. She might still experience some pain, but what were five minutes of agony in exchange for an eternity of peace? The only possible response

73

was to close her eyes: in films, the thing she most hated to see were dead people with staring eyes.

But the heart attack was different from what she had imagined; her breathing became laboured, and Veronika was horrified to realise that she was about to experience the worst of her fears: suffocation. She was going to die as if she were being buried alive, or had suddenly been plunged into the depths of the sea.

She stumbled, fell, felt a sharp blow on her face, continued making heroic efforts to breathe, but the air wouldn't go in. Worst of all, death did not come. She was entirely conscious of what was going on around her, she could still see colours and shapes, although she had difficulty in hearing what others were saying; the cries and exclamations seemed distant, as if coming from another world. Apart from this, everything else was real; the air wouldn't enter her lungs, it would simply not obey the commands of her lungs and her muscles, and still she did not lose consciousness.

She felt someone touch her and turn her over, but now she had lost control of her eye movements, and her eyes were flickering wildly, sending hundreds of different images to her brain, combining the feeling of suffocation with a sense of complete visual confusion.

After a while, the images became distant too, and just when the agony reached its peak, the air finally rushed into her lungs, making a tremendous noise that left everyone in the room paralysed with fear.

Veronika began to vomit copiously. Once the near-tragedy had passed, some of the mad people there began to laugh, and she felt humiliated, lost, paralysed.

A nurse came running in and gave her an injection in her arm.

'It's all right, calm down, it's over now.'

'I didn't die!' she started shouting, crawling towards the other patients, smearing the floor and the furniture with her vomit. 'I'm still in this bloody hospital, forced to live with you lot, living a thousand deaths every day, every night, and not one of you feels an ounce of pity for me.'

She rounded on the nurse, grabbed the syringe from his hand and threw it out into the garden.

'And what do you want? Why don't you just inject me with poison, since I'm already condemned to die? How can you be so heartless?'

Unable to control herself any longer, she sat down on the floor again and started crying uncontrollably, shouting, sobbing loudly, while some of the patients laughed and made remarks about her filthy clothes.

'Give her a sedative,' said a doctor, hurrying in. 'Get this situation under control.'

The nurse, however, was frozen to the spot. The doctor went out again and returned with two more male nurses and another syringe. The men grabbed the hysterical girl struggling in the middle of the room, while the doctor injected the last drop of sedative into a vein in her vomit-smeared arm.

She was in Dr Igor's consulting room, lying on an immaculate white bed with clean sheets on it.

He was listening to her heart. She was pretending that she was still asleep, but something inside her must have changed, judging by the doctor's muttered words:

'Don't you worry. In your state of health, you could live to be a hundred.'

Veronika opened her eyes. Someone had taken her clothes off. Who? Dr Igor? Did that mean he had seen her naked? Her brain wasn't working properly.

'What did you say?'

'I said not to worry.'

'No, you said I could live to be a hundred.'

The doctor went over to his desk.

'You said I could live to be a hundred,' Veronika repeated.

'Nothing is certain in medicine,' said Dr Igor, trying to cover up. 'Everything's possible.'

'How's my heart?'

'The same.'

She didn't need to hear any more. When faced with a serious case, doctors always say: 'You'll live to be a hundred', or 'There's nothing seriously wrong with you,' or 'You have the heart and blood pressure of a young girl,' or even 'We need to

76

redo the tests.' They're probably afraid the patient will go berserk in the consulting room.

She tried to get up, but couldn't; the whole room started to turn.

'Just lie down for a bit longer, until you feel better. You're not bothering me.'

Oh good, thought Veronika. But what if I was?

Being an experienced physician, Dr Igor remained silent for some time, pretending to be reading the papers on his desk. When we're with another person, and they say nothing, the situation becomes irritating, tense, unbearable. Dr Igor was hoping that the girl would start talking so that he could collect more data for his thesis on madness and the cure he was developing.

But Veronika didn't say a word. 'She may still be suffering from a high level of Vitriol poisoning,' thought Dr Igor, and decided to break the silence, which was becoming tense, irritating, unbearable.

'So you like to play the piano,' he said, trying to sound as nonchalant as possible.

'And the mad enjoy it too. Yesterday there was a guy listening who was utterly transfixed.'

'Yes, Eduard. He mentioned to someone how much he'd enjoyed it. Who knows, he might start eating normally again.'

'A schizophrenic liking music? And he mentioned it to someone else?'

'Yes. And I imagine you have no idea what you're talking about.'

That doctor – who looked more like a patient, with his dyed black hair – was right. Veronika had often heard the word 'schizophrenic', but she had no idea what it meant.

'Is there a cure, then?' she asked, hoping to find out more about schizophrenics.

'It can be controlled. We still don't really know what goes on in the world of madness. Everything's still so new, and the treatments change every decade or so. A schizophrenic is a person who already has a natural tendency to absent himself from this world, until some factor, sometimes serious, sometimes superficial, depending on the individual circumstances, forces him to create his own reality. It can develop into a state of complete alienation, what we call catatonia, but people do occasionally recover, at least enough to allow the patient to work and lead a near-normal life. It all depends on one thing, environment.'

'You say they create their own reality,' said Veronika, 'but what is reality?'

'It's whatever the majority deems it to be. It's not necessarily the best or the most logical, but it's the one that has become adapted to the desires of society as a whole. You see this thing I've got round my neck?'

'You mean your tie?'

'Exactly. Your answer is the logical, coherent answer an absolutely normal person would give: it's a tie! A madman, however, would say that what I have round my neck is a ridiculous, useless bit of coloured cloth tied in a very complicated way, and which makes it harder to get air into your lungs and difficult to turn your neck. I have to be careful when I'm anywhere near a fan, or I could be strangled by this bit of cloth.

'If a mad person were to ask me what this tie is for, I would have to say, absolutely nothing. It's not even purely decorative, since nowadays it's become a symbol of slavery, power, aloofness. The only really useful function a tie serves is the sense of relief when you get home and take it off; you feel as if you've freed yourself from something, though quite what you don't know.

'But does that sense of relief justify the existence of ties? No. Nevertheless, if I were to ask a madman and a normal person what this is, the sane person would say: a tie. It doesn't matter who's correct, what matters is who's right.'

'So just because I gave the right name to a bit of coloured cloth you conclude that I'm not mad.'

No, you're not mad, thought Dr Igor, who was an authority on the subject, with various diplomas hung on the walls of his consulting room. Attempting to take your own life was something proper to a human being; he knew a lot of people who were doing just that, and yet they lived outside the hospital, feigning innocence and normality, merely because they had not chosen the scandalous route of suicide. They were killing themselves gradually, poisoning themselves with what Dr Igor called Vitriol.

Vitriol was a toxic substance, whose symptoms he had identified in his conversations with the men and women he had met. Now he was writing a thesis on the subject, which he would submit to the Slovenian Academy of Sciences for their scrutiny. It was the most important step in the field of insanity since Dr Pinel had ordered that patients should be unshackled, astonishing the medical world with the idea that some of them might even be cured.

As with the libido – the chemical reaction responsible for sexual desire which Dr Freud had identified, but which no laboratory had ever managed to isolate – Vitriol was released by the human organism whenever a person found him or herself in a frightening situation, although it had yet to be picked up in any spectrographic tests. It was easily recognised, though, by its taste, which was neither sweet nor savoury – a bitter taste. Dr Igor, the as yet unrecognised discoverer of this fatal substance, had given it the name of a poison much favoured in the past by emperors, kings and lovers of all kinds whenever they needed to rid themselves of some obstructive person.

A golden age, the age of kings and emperors, when you could live and die romantically. The murderer would invite his or her victim to partake of a magnificent supper, the servant would pour them drinks served in two exquisite glasses, and one of the drinks would be laced with Vitriol. Imagine the excitement aroused by each gesture the victim made, picking up the glass, saying a few tender or aggressive words, drinking as if the glass contained some delicious beverage, giving his host one last startled look, then falling to the floor.

But this poison, which was now very expensive and difficult to obtain, had been replaced by more reliable methods of extermination – revolvers, bacteria, etc. Dr Igor, a natural romantic, had rescued this name from obscurity and given it to the disease of the soul he had managed to diagnose, and whose discovery would soon amaze the world.

It was odd that no one had ever described Vitriol as a mortal poison, although most of the people affected could identify its taste, and they referred to the process of poisoning as Bitterness. To a greater or lesser degree, everyone had some Bitterness in their organism, just as we are all carriers of the tuberculosis bacillus. But these two illnesses only attack when the patient is debilitated; in the case of Bitterness, the right conditions for the disease occur when the person becomes afraid of so-called 'reality'.

Certain people, in their eagerness to construct a world which no external threat can penetrate, build exaggeratedly high defences against the outside world, against new people, new places, different experiences, and leave their inner world stripped bare. It is there that Bitterness begins its irrevocable work.

The will was the main target of Bitterness (or Vitriol, as Dr Igor preferred to call it). The people attacked by this malaise began to lose all desire, and, within a few years, they became unable to leave their world, where they had spent enormous reserves of energy constructing high walls in order to make reality what they wanted it to be.

In order to avoid external attack, they had also deliberately limited internal growth. They continued going to work, watching television, having children, complaining about the traffic, but these things happened automatically, unaccompanied by any particular emotion, because, after all, everything was under control.

The great problem with poisoning by Bitterness was that the passions – hatred, love, despair, enthusiasm, curiosity – also ceased to manifest themselves. After a while, the embittered person felt no desire at all. They lacked the will either to live or to die, that was the problem.

That is why embittered people find heroes and madmen a perennial source of fascination, for they have no fear of life or death. Both heroes and madmen are indifferent to danger and will forge ahead regardless of what other people say. The madman committed suicide, the hero offered himself up to martyrdom in the name of a cause, but both would die, and the embittered would spend many nights and days remarking on the absurdity and the glory of both. It was the only moment when the embittered person had the energy to clamber up his defensive walls and peer over at the world outside, but then his hands and feet would grow tired and he would return to daily life.

The chronically embittered person only noticed his illness once a week, on Sunday afternoons. Then, with no work or routine to relieve the symptoms, he would feel that something was very wrong, since he found the peace of those endless after-noons infernal and felt only a keen sense of constant irritation.

Monday would arrive, however, and the embittered man would immediately forget his symptoms, although he would curse the fact that he never had time to rest and would com-plain that the weekends always passed far too quickly.

From the social point of view, the only advantage of the disease was that it had become the norm, and internment was no longer necessary, except in cases where the poisoning was so serious that the patient's behaviour began to affect others. Most embittered people, though, could continue to live outside, con-stituting no threat to society or to others, since, because of the high walls with which they had surrounded themselves, they were totally isolated from the world, even though they appeared to participate in it.

Dr Sigmund Freud had discovered the libido and a cure for the problems it caused, in the form of psychoanalysis. Apart from discovering the existence of Vitriol, Dr Igor needed to prove that a cure for it was also possible. He wanted to leave his mark on the history of medicine, although he had no illu-sions about the difficulties he would face when it came to pub-lishing his ideas, for 'normal' people were contented with their lives and would never admit to the existence of such an illness, whilst the 'sick' fed a gigantic industry of mental hospitals, lab-oratories, congresses, etc.

'I know the world will not recognise my efforts,' he said to himself, proud of being misunderstood. After all, that was the price every genius had to pay.

'Is there anything wrong, doctor?' asked the girl. 'You seem to have drifted off into the world of your patients.'

Dr Igor ignored the disrespectful comment.

'You can go now,' he said.

Veronika didn't know if it was day or night. Dr Igor had the light on, but then he did every morning. It was only when she reached the corridor and saw the moon that she realised she had slept far longer than she had thought.

On the way to the ward, she noticed a framed photograph on the wall: it was of the main square in Ljubljana, before the statue of the poet Prešeren had been put up; it showed couples strolling, probably on a Sunday.

She looked at the date on the photograph: the summer of 1910.

The summer of 1910. There were all those people, whose children and grandchildren had already died, frozen in one particular moment of their lives. The women wore voluminous dresses and the men were all wearing hat, jacket, gaiters, tie (or that coloured piece of cloth as the mad call it) and carrying an umbrella under one arm.

And how hot would it have been then? The temperature must have been what it would be today in summer, thirty-five degrees in the shade. If an Englishman turned up in clothing more suited to the heat – in Bermuda shorts and shirtsleeves – what would those people think?

'He must be mad.'

She had understood perfectly what Dr Igor meant, just as

she understood that, although she had always felt loved and protected, there had been one missing element that would have transformed that love into a blessing: she should have allowed herself to be a little madder.

Her parents would still have loved her, but, afraid of hurting them, she had not dared to pay the price of her dream, the dream that was buried in the depths of her memory, although sometimes it was awoken by a concert or by a beautiful record she happened to hear. Whenever her dream was awoken, though, the feeling of frustration was so intense that she immediately sent it back to sleep again.

Veronika had known since childhood that her true vocation was to be a pianist.

This was something she had felt ever since her first lesson, at twelve. Her teacher had recognised her talent too and had encouraged her to become a professional. However, whenever she had felt pleased about a competition she had just won and said to her mother that she intended giving up everything and dedicating herself to the piano, her mother would look at her fondly and say: 'No one makes a living playing the piano, my love.'

'But you were the one who wanted me to have lessons.'

'To develop your artistic gifts, that's all. A husband likes that kind of thing in a wife; he can show you off at parties. Forget about being a pianist, and go and study law, that's the profession of the future.'

Veronika did as her mother asked, sure that her mother had enough experience of life to understand reality. She finished her studies, went to university, got a good degree, but ended up working as a librarian.

'I should have been madder.' But, as doubtless happens with most people, she had found this out too late.

She was about to continue on her way, when someone took her by the arm. The powerful sedative was still flowing in her veins; that's why she didn't react when Eduard, the schizophrenic, delicately began to lead her in a different direction – towards the lounge.

The moon was still new and Veronika had already sat down at the piano – in response to Eduard's silent request – when she heard a voice coming from the refectory, someone speaking with a foreign accent which Veronika could not remember having heard in Villete before.

'I don't want to play the piano just now, Eduard. I want to know what's going on in the world, what they're talking about over there, who that man is.'

Eduard smiled, perhaps not understanding a word she was saying, but she remembered what Dr Igor had said: schizophrenics could move in and out of their separate realities.

'I'm going to die,' she went on, hoping that her words were making sense to him. 'Today, death brushed my face with its wing and will probably be knocking at my door if not tomorrow, then soon afterwards. It's not a good idea for you to get used to listening to the piano every night.

'No one should let themselves get used to anything, Eduard. Look at me, I was beginning to enjoy the sun again, the mountains, even life's problems, I was beginning to accept that the meaninglessness of life was no one's fault but mine. I wanted to see the main square in Ljubljana again, to feel hatred and love, despair and tedium, all those simple, foolish things that make up everyday life, but which give pleasure to your existence. If one day I could get out of here, I would allow myself to be mad, because everyone is, indeed, the maddest are the ones who don't know they're mad, but keep repeating what others tell them to.

'But none of that's possible, do you see? In the same way, you can't spend the whole day waiting for night to come and for one of the patients to play the piano, because soon that will end. My world and yours are about to come to an end.'

She got up, tenderly touched the boy's face and then went to the refectory.

When she opened the door, she came upon an unusual scene; the tables and chairs had been pushed back against the walls, forming a large central space. There, sitting on the floor, were the members of the Fraternity, listening to a man in a suit and tie.

'...then they invited Nasrudin, the great master of the Sufi tradition, to give a lecture,' he was saying.

When the door opened, everyone in the room looked at Veronika. The man in the suit turned to her.

'Sit down.'

She sat down on the floor, next to Mari, the white-haired woman who had been so aggressive on their first encounter. To Veronika's surprise, Mari gave her a welcoming smile.

The man in the suit went on:

'Nasrudin arranged to give a lecture at two o'clock in the afternoon, and it looked set to be a great success: the thousand seats were completely sold out and more than seven hundred people were left outside, watching the lecture on closed-circuit television.

'At two o'clock precisely, an assistant of Nasrudin's came in, saying that, for unavoidable reasons, the lecture would begin late. Some got up indignantly, asked for their money back and left. Even so, a lot of people remained both inside and outside the lecture hall.

'By four in the afternoon, the Sufi master had still not

appeared and people gradually began to leave the place, picking up their money at the box office. The working day was coming to an end, it was time to go home. When it was six o'clock, the original one thousand seven hundred spectators had dwindled to less than a hundred.

'At that moment, Nasrudin came in. He appeared to be extremely drunk and began to flirt with a beautiful young woman sitting in the front row.

'Astonished, the people who had remained behind began to feel indignant. How could the man behave like that after making them wait four solid hours? There were some disapproving murmurs, but the Sufi master ignored them. He went on, in a loud voice, to say how sexy the young woman was, and invited her to go with him to France.'

Some teacher, thought Veronika. Just as well I've never believed in such things.

'After cursing the people who were complaining, Nasrudin tried to get up, but fell heavily to the floor. Disgusted, more people decided to leave, saying it was pure charlatanism, that they would denounce the degrading spectacle to the press.

'Only nine people remained. As soon as the final group of outraged spectators had left, Nasrudin got up; he was completely sober, his eyes glowed, and he had about him an air of great authority and wisdom. "Those of you who stayed are the ones who will hear me," he said. "You have passed through the two hardest tests on the spiritual road: the patience to wait for the right moment and the courage not to be disappointed with what you encounter. It is you I will teach."

'And Nasrudin shared with them some of the Sufi techniques.'

The man paused and took a strange flute out of his pocket.

'Let's take a short break now, and then we'll do our meditation.'

The members of the group stood up. Veronika didn't know what to do.

'You get up too,' said Mari, grabbing her hand. 'We've got a five-minute break.'

'I'll leave, I don't want to be in the way.'

Mari led her to one corner.

'Haven't you learned anything, not even with the approach of death? Stop thinking all the time that you're in the way, that you're bothering the person next to you. If people don't like it, they can complain. And if they don't have the courage to complain, that's their problem.'

'That day, when I came over to you, I was doing something I'd never dared to do before.'

'And you allowed yourself to be cowed by a joke made by a mad person. Why didn't you just stick to your guns? What did you have to lose?'

'My dignity, by being where I wasn't welcome.'

'What's dignity? It's wanting everyone to think you're good, well-behaved, full of love for your fellow man. Have some respect for nature, watch a few films about animals and see how they fight for their own space. We all heartily approved of that slap of yours.'

Veronika did not have any more time to spend fighting for space, and so she changed the subject and asked who the man in the suit was.

'You're improving,' laughed Mari. 'You now ask questions without worrying about whether you're being indiscreet or not. He's a Sufi master.'

'What does Sufi mean?'

'Wool.'

Veronika didn't understand. Wool?

'Sufism is the spiritual tradition of the dervishes. Its teachers never strive to show how wise they are, and their disciples go into a trance by performing a kind of whirling dance.'

'What's the point of that?'

'I'm not quite sure, but our group has resolved to investigate all prohibited experiences. All my life, the government taught us that the only purpose of searching for a spiritual meaning to life was to make people forget about their real problems. Now tell me this: wouldn't you say that trying to understand life was a real problem?'

Yes, it was, although Veronika wasn't sure any more what the word 'real' meant.

The man in the suit – a Sufi master, according to Mari – asked them all to sit in a circle. From a vase he removed all the flowers but one, a single red rose, and this he placed in the centre of the group.

'You see how far we've come,' said Veronika to Mari. 'Some madman decided it was possible to grow flowers in winter, and nowadays, throughout Europe, we have roses all year round. Do you think even a Sufi master, with all his knowledge, could do that?'

Mari seemed to guess her thoughts.

'Save your criticisms for later.'

'I'll try to, although all I have is the present, and a very brief one too it seems.'

'That's all anyone has, and it's always very brief, although, of course, some people believe they have a past where they can accumulate things and a future where they will accumulate still more. By the way, speaking of the present moment, do you masturbate a lot?'

Although still under the effects of the sedative she had been given, Veronika was immediately reminded of the first words she had heard in Villete.

'When I was first brought here and was still full of tubes

from the artificial respirator, I clearly heard someone asking me if I wanted to be masturbated. What *is* all that about? Why do you people spend your time thinking about such things?'

'It's the same outside; it's just that here we don't need to hide the fact.'

'Was it you who asked me?'

'No, but I think that, as far as pleasure is concerned, you do need to discover how far you can go. Next time, with a little patience, you might be able to take your partner there too, instead of waiting to be guided by him. Even if you have only got two days to live, I don't think you should leave this life without knowing how far you can go.'

'Only if my partner is the schizophrenic who's right now waiting to hear me play the piano again.'

'He's certainly nice-looking.'

The man in the suit interrupted their conversation with a call for silence. He told everyone to concentrate on the rose and to empty their minds.

'The thoughts will come back, but try to push them to one side. You have two choices: to control your mind or to let your mind control you. You're already familiar with the latter experience, allowing yourself to be swept along by fears, neuroses, insecurity, for we all have self-destructive tendencies.

'Don't confuse madness with a loss of control. Remember that in the Sufi tradition, the master – Nasrudin – is the one everyone calls the madman. And it is precisely because his fellow citizens consider him mad that Nasrudin can say whatever he thinks and do whatever he wants. So it was with court jesters in the Middle Ages; they could alert the king to dangers that the ministers would not dare to comment upon, because they were afraid of losing their positions.

'That's how it should be with you; stay mad, but behave like normal people. Run the risk of being different, but learn to do so without attracting attention. Concentrate on this flower and allow the real "I" to reveal itself.'

'What is the real "I"?' asked Veronika. Perhaps everyone else there knew, but what did it matter: she must learn to care less about annoying others.

The man seemed surprised by the interruption, but he answered her question.

'It's what you are, not what others make of you.'

Veronika decided to do the exercise, concentrating as hard as she could on discovering who she was. During those days in Villete, she had felt things she had never before felt with such intensity – hatred, love, fear, curiosity, a desire to live. Perhaps Mari was right: did she really know what it meant to have an orgasm? Or had she only gone as far as men had wanted to take her?

The man started playing the flute. Gradually the music calmed her soul, and she managed to concentrate on the rose. It might have been the effect of the sedative, but the fact was that since she had left Dr Igor's consulting room, she had felt extremely well.

She knew she was going to die soon, why be afraid? It wouldn't help at all, it wouldn't avoid the fatal heart attack; the best plan would be to enjoy the days and hours that remained to her, doing things she had never done before.

The music was soft, and the dim light in the refectory created an almost religious atmosphere. Religion: why didn't she try going deep inside herself and see what remained of her beliefs and her faith?

The music, however, was leading her elsewhere: empty your mind, stop thinking about anything, simply BE. Veronika gave herself up to the experience; she stared at the rose, saw who she was, liked what she saw and felt only regret that she had been so hasty.

When the meditation was over and the Sufi master had left, Mari stayed on for a while in the refectory, talking to the other members of the Fraternity. Veronika said she was tired and left at once; after all, the sedative she had been given that morning had been strong enough to knock out a horse, and yet she had still had strength enough to remain awake all that time.

'That's youth for you; it sets its own limits without even asking if the body can take it. Yet the body always does.'

Mari wasn't tired; she had slept until late, then decided to go for a walk in Ljubljana – Dr Igor required that the members of the Fraternity left Villete every day. She had gone to the cinema and fallen asleep again in her seat, watching a deeply boring film about marital conflict. Was there no other subject? Why always repeat the same stories – husband with lover, husband with wife and sick child, husband with wife, lover and sick child? There were more important things in the world to talk about.

The conversation in the refectory did not last long; the meditation had left the group members feeling relaxed and they were all ready to go back to their wards, apart from Mari, who instead went out into the garden. On the way, she passed the lounge and saw that the young woman had not yet managed to get to bed.

She was playing for Eduard the schizophrenic, who had perhaps been waiting all that time by the piano. Like children, the mad will not budge until their desires have been satisfied.

The air was icy. Mari came back in, grabbed a coat and went out again. Outside, far from the eyes of everyone, she lit a cigarette. She smoked slowly and guiltlessly, thinking about the young woman, the piano music she could hear and life outside the walls of Villete, which was becoming unbearably difficult for everyone.

In Mari's view, this difficulty was due not to chaos or disorganisation or anarchy, but to an excess of order. Society had more and more rules, and laws that contradicted the rules, and new rules that contradicted the laws. People felt too frightened to take even a step outside the invisible regulations that guided everyone's lives.

Mari knew what she was talking about; until her illness had brought her to Villete, she had spent forty years of her life working as a lawyer. She had lost her innocent vision of Justice early on in her career, and had come to understand that the laws had not been created to resolve problems, but in order to prolong quarrels indefinitely.

It was a shame that Allah, Jehovah, God – it didn't matter what name you gave him – did not live in the world today, because if He did, we would still be in Paradise, while He would be mired in appeals, requests, demands, injunctions, preliminary verdicts, and would have to justify to innumerable tribunals His decision to expel Adam and Eve from Paradise for breaking an arbitrary rule with no foundation in law: Of the tree of the knowledge of good and evil thou shalt not eat.

If he had not wanted that to happen, why did he put the tree in the midst of the garden and not outside the walls of

Paradise? If she were called upon to defend the couple, Mari would undoubtedly accuse God of administrative negligence, because, as well as planting the tree in the wrong place, he had failed to surround it with warnings and barriers, had failed to adopt even minimal security arrangements, and had thus exposed everyone to danger.

Mari could also accuse him of inducement to criminal activity, for he had pointed out to Adam and Eve the exact place where the tree was to be found. If he had said nothing, generation upon generation would have passed on this earth without anyone taking the slightest interest in the forbidden fruit, since the tree was presumably in a forest full of similar trees, and therefore of no particular value.

But God had proceeded quite differently. He had devised a rule and then found a way of persuading someone to break it, merely in order to invent Punishment. He knew that Adam and Eve would become bored with perfection and would, sooner or later, test His patience. He set a trap, perhaps because He, Almighty God, was also bored with everything going so smoothly: if Eve had not eaten the apple, nothing of any interest would have happened in the last few billion years.

When the law was broken, God – the Omnipotent Judge – even pretended to pursue them, as if he did not already know every possible hiding place. With the angels looking on, amused by the game (life must have been very dreary for them since Lucifer left Heaven), he began to walk about the garden. Mari thought what a wonderful scene in a suspense movie that episode from the Bible would make: God's footsteps, the couple exchanging frightened glances, the feet suddenly stopping by their hiding place.

'Where art thou?' asked God.

'I heard thy voice in the garden, and I was afraid, because I was naked; and I hid myself,' Adam replied, without knowing that by making this statement, he had confessed himself guilty of a crime.

So, by means of a simple trick, pretending not to know where Adam was nor why he had run away, God got what he wanted. Even so, in order to leave no doubts amongst the audience of angels who were intently watching the episode, he decided to go further.

'Who told thee that thou was naked?' said God, knowing that this question could have only one possible response: because I ate of the tree of the knowledge of good and evil.

With that question, God demonstrated to his angels that he was a just god, and that his condemnation of the couple was based on solid evidence. From then on, it wasn't a matter of whether it was the woman's fault or of their asking for forgiveness: God needed an example, so that no other being, earthly or heavenly, would ever again dare to go against his decisions.

God expelled the couple, and their children paid for the crime too (as still happens with the children of criminals) and thus the judiciary system was invented: the law, the transgression of the law (no matter how illogical or absurd), judgement (in which the more experienced triumphs over the ingenuous) and punishment.

Since all of humanity was condemned with no right of appeal, humankind decided to create a defence mechanism, against the eventuality of God deciding to wield his arbitrary power again. However, millennia of study resulted in so many legal measures that, ultimately, we went too far, and justice became a tangle of clauses, jurisprudence and contradictory texts that no one could quite understand.

So much so that, when God had a change of heart and sent His Son to save the world, what happened? He fell into the hands of the very justice He had invented.

The tangle of laws created such confusion that the Son ended up nailed to a cross. It was no simple trial; he was passed from Ananias to Caiphas, from the priest to Pilate, who alleged that there were insufficient laws in the Roman code. From Pilate to Herod, who, in turn, alleged that the Jewish code did not permit the death sentence. From Herod back to Pilate again, who, looking for a way out, offered the people a juridical deal: he had the Son beaten and then displayed to the people with his wounds, but it didn't work.

Like prosecutors nowadays, Pilate decided to save himself at the expense of the condemned man: he offered to exchange Jesus for Barabbas, knowing that, by then, justice had become a grand spectacle requiring a denouement: the death of the prisoner.

Finally, Pilate used the article of law that gave the judge, and not the person being judged, the benefit of the doubt. He washed his hands, which means: 'I'm not quite sure either way.' It was just another ruse to preserve the Roman juridical system without injuring relations with local magistrates, and even transferring the weight of the decision onto the people, just in case the sentence should cause any problems, and some inspector from the imperial capital came to see for himself what was going on.

Justice. Law. Although both were vital in order to protect the innocent, they did not always work to everyone's liking. Mari was glad to be far from all that confusion, although tonight, listening to the piano, she was not quite so sure that Villete was the right place for her.

'If I were to decide once and for all to leave here, I wouldn't go back to the law. I'm not going to spend my time with mad people who think they're normal and important, but whose sole function in life is to make everything more difficult for others. I'll be a seamstress, an embroiderer, I'll sell fruit outside the Municipal Theatre. I've already made my contribution to the futile madness of the law.'

In Villete you were allowed to smoke, but not to stub your cigarette out on the lawn. With great pleasure, she did what was forbidden, because the great advantage of being there was not having to respect the rules and not even having to put up with any major consequences if you broke them.

She went over to the door. The guard – there was always a guard there, after all, that was the law – nodded to her and opened the door.

'I'm not going out,' she said.

'Lovely piano music,' said the guard. 'I've listened to it nearly every night.'

'It won't last much longer,' she said and walked rapidly away so as not to have to explain.

She remembered what she had read in the young girl's eyes the moment she had come into the refectory: fear.

Fear. Veronika might feel insecurity, shyness, shame, constraint, but why fear? That was only justifiable when confronted by a real threat: ferocious animals, armed attackers, earthquakes, but not a group of people gathered together in a refectory.

'But human beings are like that,' she said. 'We've replaced nearly all our emotions with fear.'

And Mari knew what she was talking about, because that was what had brought her to Villete: panic attacks.

In her room Mari had a veritable library of articles on the subject. Now people talked about it openly, and she had recently seen a German television programme in which people discussed their experiences. In that same programme, a survey revealed that a significant percentage of the population suffers from panic attacks, although most of those affected tried to hide the symptoms, for fear of being considered mad.

But at the time when Mari had her first attack, none of this was known. 'It was absolute hell,' she thought, lighting another cigarette.

The piano was still playing, the girl seemed to have enough energy to play all night.

A lot of the inmates had been affected by the young woman's arrival in the hospital, Mari amongst them. At first, she had tried to avoid her, afraid to awaken the young woman's desire to live; since there was no escape, it was better that she should keep on wanting to die. Dr Igor had let it be known that, even though she would continue to be given daily injections, her physical condition would visibly deteriorate and there would be no way of saving her.

The inmates had understood the message and kept their distance from the condemned woman. However, without anyone knowing quite why, Veronika had begun fighting for her life, and the only two people who approached her were Zedka, who would be leaving tomorrow and didn't talk that much anyway, and Eduard.

Mari needed to have a word with Eduard; he always respected her opinions. Did he not realise he was drawing Veronika back into the world, and that that was the worst thing he could do to someone with no hope of salvation?

She considered a thousand ways of explaining the situation

to him, but all of them would only make him feel guilty, and that she would never do. Mari thought a little and decided to let things run their normal course. She was no longer a lawyer and she did not want to set a bad example by creating new behaviour laws in a place where anarchy should reign.

But the presence of the young woman had touched a lot of people there, and some were ready to rethink their lives. At one of the meetings with the Fraternity, someone had tried to explain what was happening. Deaths in Villete tended to happen suddenly, without giving anyone time to think about it, or after a long illness, when death is always a blessing.

The young woman's case, though, was dramatic because she was so young and because she now wanted to live again, something they all knew to be impossible. Some people asked themselves 'What if that happened to me? I do have a chance to live. Am I making good use of it?'

Some were not bothered with finding an answer; they had long ago given up and now formed part of a world in which neither life nor death, space or time existed. Others, however, were being forced to think hard, and Mari was one of them.

Veronika stopped playing for a moment and looked out at Mari in the garden. She was wearing only a light jacket against the cold night air; did she want to die?

'No, I was the one who wanted to die.'

She turned back to the piano. In the last days of her life, she had finally realised her grand dream: to play with heart and soul, for as long as she wanted and whenever the mood took her. It didn't matter to her that her only audience was a young schizophrenic; he seemed to understand the music, and that was what mattered.

Mari had never wanted to kill herself. On the contrary, five years before, in the same cinema she had visited today, she had watched, horrified, a film about poverty in El Salvador and thought how important her life was. At that time – with her children grown up and making their way in their own professions – she had decided to give up the tedious, unending job of being a lawyer in order to dedicate the rest of her days to working for some humanitarian organisation. The rumours of civil war in the country were growing all the time, but Mari didn't believe them. It was impossible that, at the end of the twentieth century, the European Community would allow a new war at their gates.

On the other side of the world, however, there was no shortage of tragedies, and one of those tragedies was El Salvador's, where starving children were forced to live on the streets and turn to prostitution.

'It's terrible,' she said to her husband, who was sitting in the seat next to her.

He nodded.

Mari had been putting off the decision for a long time, but perhaps now was the moment to talk to him. They had been given all the good things that life could possibly offer them: a home, work, good children, modest comforts, interests and culture. Why not do something for others for a change? Mari had contacts in the Red Cross and she knew that volunteers were desperately needed in many parts of the world.

She was tired of struggling with bureaucracy and law suits, unable to help people who had spent years of their lives trying to resolve problems not of their own making. Working with the Red Cross, though, she would see immediate results.

She decided that, when they left the cinema, she would invite her husband for a coffee so that they could discuss the idea.

Just as a Salvadorean government official appeared on screen to offer a bored excuse for some new injustice, Mari suddenly noticed her heart beating faster.

She told herself it was nothing. Perhaps the stuffy atmosphere in the cinema was getting to her; if the symptoms persisted she would go out to the foyer to get a breath of fresh air.

But events took on their own momentum; her heart began beating faster and faster, and she broke out in a cold sweat.

She felt afraid and tried hard to concentrate on the film, in an attempt to dispel any negative thoughts, but realised she could no longer follow what was happening on the screen. Mari could see the images and the subtitles, but she seemed to have entered a completely different reality, where everything going on around her seemed strange and out of kilter, as if taking place in a world she did not know.

'I don't feel well,' she said to her husband.

She had put off making that remark as long as possible, because it meant admitting that there was something wrong, but she could not hold out any longer.

'Let's go outside,' he said.

When he took his wife's hand to help her to her feet, he noticed it was ice cold.

'I don't think I can get that far. Please, tell me what's happening to me.'

Her husband felt afraid too. Sweat was pouring down Mari's face and there was a strange light in her eyes.

'Keep calm. I'll go out and call a doctor.'

She was gripped by despair. What he said made absolute sense, but everything – the cinema, the semi-darkness, the people sitting side by side staring up at the brilliant screen – all of it seemed so threatening. She was certain she was alive, she could even touch the life around her as if it were something solid. And that had never happened to her before.

'On no account leave me here alone. I'll get up and go out with you, but take it slowly.'

They both made their apologies to the people in the same row as them, and began walking to the exit at the back of the cinema. Mari's heart was now beating furiously, and she was certain, absolutely certain, that she would never get out of that place. Everything she did, every gesture she made – placing one foot in front of the other, saying 'excuse me', holding on to her husband's arm, breathing in and out – seemed terrifyingly conscious and deliberate.

She had never felt so frightened in her life.

'I'm going to die right here in this cinema.'

And she was convinced she knew what was happening, because, many years before, a friend of hers had died in a cinema of a cerebral aneurism.

Cerebral aneurisms are like time bombs. They are tiny varicose veins that form along the arteries – like the ballooning you get on worn tyres – and they can remain there undetected during a whole lifetime. No one knows if they've got an aneurism, unless it's discovered accidentally, for example, after a brain scan carried out for other reasons, or at the moment when it actually ruptures, flooding everything with blood, leaving the person in an immediate state of coma, usually followed shortly by death.

While she was walking down the aisle of the dark cinema, Mari remembered the friend she had lost. The strangest thing, though, was the effect this ruptured aneurism was having on her perception. She seemed to have been transported to a different planet, seeing each familiar thing as if for the first time.

And then there was the terrifying, inexplicable fear, the sheer panic of being alone on that other planet. Death.

'I must stop thinking. I'll pretend that everything's all right and then everything will be.'

She tried to act naturally and, for a few seconds, the sense of oddness diminished. The two minutes that elapsed between first feeling the palpitations and reaching the exit with her husband were the most terrifying two minutes of her life.

When they reached the brightly-lit foyer, however, everything seemed to start up again. The colours were so garish, the noises from the street seemed to rush in on her from all sides, and everything seemed utterly unreal. She started to notice certain details for the first time, for example, the clarity of vision that covers only the small area on which we fix our gaze, while the rest remains completely unfocused.

There was more. She knew that everything she could see around her was just a scene created by electrical impulses inside her brain, using light impulses that passed through a gelatinous organ called the eye.

No, she must stop thinking. That way madness lay.

By then, her fear of an aneurism had passed; she had managed to get out of the cinema and was still alive. The friend who had died, on the other hand, never even had time to leave her seat.

'I'll call an ambulance,' said her husband, when he saw his wife's ashen face and bloodless lips.

'Call a taxi,' she said, hearing the sounds leaving her mouth, conscious of the vibration of each vocal cord.

Going to hospital would mean accepting that she really was seriously ill and Mari was determined to do her utmost to restore everything to normality.

They left the foyer, and the icy cold air seemed to have a positive effect; Mari recovered some control over herself, although the inexplicable feelings of panic and terror persisted. While her husband was desperately trying to find a taxi, which were scarce at that time of day, she sat down on the kerb and tried not to look at her surroundings: the children playing, the buses passing, the music coming from a nearby funfair, all seemed absolutely surreal, frightening, alien.

Finally, a taxi appeared.

'To the hospital,' said her husband, helping his wife in.

'Please, let's just go home,' she said. She didn't want any more strange places, she was desperately in need of familiar, ordinary things that might diminish the fear she was feeling.

While the taxi was driving them home, her heart rate gradually slowed and her temperature began to return to normal.

'I'm beginning to feel better,' she said to her husband. 'It must have been something I ate.'

When they reached home, the world again seemed exactly as it had been since her childhood. When she saw her husband go over to the phone, she asked him what he was doing.

'I'm going to call a doctor.'

'There's no need. Look at me, I'm fine.'

The colour had returned to her cheeks, her heart was beating normally and the uncontrollable fear had vanished.

Mari slept heavily that night and woke convinced that someone must have put some drug in the coffee they had drunk before they went into the cinema. It was a dangerous prank, and she was fully prepared, at the end of the afternoon, to call the prosecutor and go to the bar to try and find the person responsible.

She went to work, read through several pending law suits and tried to occupy herself with various other tasks, for the experience of the previous day had left a residue of fear, and she wanted to prove to herself that it would never happen again.

She discussed the film on El Salvador with one of her colleagues and mentioned in passing that she was fed up with doing the same thing every day.

'Perhaps it's time I retired.'

'You're one of the best lawyers we've got,' said the colleague. 'Besides, law is one of the few professions where age is in your favour. Why not take a long holiday instead? I'm sure you'd come back to work with renewed energy.'

'I want to do something completely different with my life. I want to have an adventure, help other people, do something I've never done before.'

The conversation ended there. She went down to the square, had lunch in a more expensive restaurant than the one she normally went to, and returned to the office early. That moment marked the beginning of her withdrawal.

The rest of the employees had still not come back, and Mari took the opportunity to look over the work still on her desk. She opened the drawer to take out the pencil which she always kept in the same place and she couldn't find it. For a fraction of a second, it occurred to her that her failure to put the pencil back in its proper place was an indication that she was perhaps behaving oddly.

That was enough to make her heart start pounding again, and the terror of the previous night returned in force.

Mari was frozen to the spot. The sun was coming in through the shutters, lending a brighter, more aggressive tone to everything about her, but she again had the feeling that she was about to die at any minute. It was all so strange; what was she doing in that office?

'I don't believe in you, God, but please, help me.'

Again she broke out in a cold sweat and realised that she was unable to control her fear. If someone came in at that moment, they would notice her frightened eyes and she would be lost.

'Cold air.'

The cold air had made her feel better the previous night, but how could she get as far as the street? Once more she was noticing each detail of what was happening to her – her breathing rate (there were moments when she felt that if she did not make a special effort to inhale and exhale, her body would be incapable of doing so itself), the movement of her head (the images succeeded each other as if there were television cameras whirring inside it), her heart beating faster and faster, her body bathed in a cold, sticky sweat.

And then the terror, an awful, inexplicable fear of doing anything, of taking a single step, of leaving the chair she was sitting in.

'It will pass.'

It had passed last time, but now she was at work, what could she do? She looked at the clock and it seemed to her an absurd mechanism, two needles turning on the same axis, indicating a measurement of time that no one had ever explained: why twelve and not ten, like all our other measurements?

'I mustn't think about these things, they make me crazy.'

Crazy. Perhaps that was the right word to describe what was wrong with her. Summoning all her willpower, she got to her feet and made her way to the toilets. Fortunately, the office was still empty and, in a minute that seemed to last an eternity, she managed to reach them. She splashed her face with water, and the feeling of strangeness diminished, although the fear remained.

'It will pass,' she said to herself. 'Yesterday it did.'

She remembered that, the day before, the whole thing had lasted about thirty minutes. She locked herself in one of the toilets, sat on the toilet seat and put her head between her knees. That position, however, seemed only to amplify the sound of her heart beating and Mari immediately sat up again.

'It will pass.'

She stayed there, thinking that she no longer knew who she was, that she was hopelessly lost. She heard the sound of people coming in and out of the toilets, taps being turned on and off, pointless conversations about banal subjects. More than once someone tried to open the door of the cubicle where she was sitting, but she said something in a murmur and no one insisted. The noise of toilets flushing was like some horrendous force of nature, capable of demolishing an entire building and sweeping everyone down into hell.

But, as she had foreseen, the fear passed off and her heartbeat returned to normal. It was just as well that her secretary was incompetent enough not even to notice her absence, otherwise the whole office would have been in the toilets asking if she was all right.

When she saw that she had regained control of herself, Mari opened the cubicle door, again splashed her face with water for a long time and went back to the office.

'You haven't got any make-up on,' said a trainee. 'Do you want to borrow some of mine?'

Mari didn't even bother to reply. She went into the office, picked up her handbag and her personal belongings, and told her secretary that she would be spending the rest of the day at home.

'But you've got loads of appointments,' protested her secretary.

'You don't give orders, you receive them. Do exactly as I say, and cancel the appointments.'

The secretary stared at this woman with whom she had been working for nearly three years, and who had never once been rude to her before. Something must be seriously wrong with her, perhaps someone had told her that her husband was at home with his lover, and she wanted to catch them *in flagrante*.

'She's a good lawyer, she knows what she's doing,' said the girl to herself. Doubtless tomorrow she would come and apologise to her.

There was no tomorrow. That night, Mari had a long conversation with her husband and described all the symptoms she had experienced. Together, they reached the conclusion that the palpitations, the cold sweats, the feelings of displacement, impotence, lack of control, could all be summed up in one word: fear. Together, husband and wife pondered what was happening. He thought it might be a brain tumour, but he didn't say anything. She thought she was having premonitions of some terrible event, but she didn't say anything either. They tried to find some common ground for discussion, like logical, reasonable, mature people.

'Perhaps you'd better have some tests done.'

Mari agreed, on one condition, that no one, not even their children, should know anything about it.

The next day she applied for and was given thirty days' unpaid leave from the office. Her husband thought of taking her to Austria where there were many eminent specialists in disorders of the brain, but she refused to leave the house; the attacks were becoming more frequent and lasted longer.

With great difficulty, with Mari dosed up on tranquillisers, the two of them managed to get as far as a hospital in Ljubljana where Mari underwent a vast range of tests. Nothing unusual was found, not even an aneurism – a source of consolation to Mari for the rest of her life.

The panic attacks continued however. While her husband did the shopping and the cooking, Mari obsessively cleaned the house every day, just to keep her mind fixed on other things. She started reading all the psychiatry books she could find, only immediately to put them down again because she seemed to recognise her own malaise in each of the illnesses they described.

The worst of it was that, although the attacks were no longer a novelty, she still felt the same intense fear and sense of alienation from reality, the same loss of self-control. In addition, she started to feel guilty about her husband, obliged to do his own job as well as all the housework, cleaning apart.

As time passed, and the situation remained unresolved, Mari began to feel and express a deep irritation. The slightest thing made her lose her temper and start shouting, then sob hysterically.

After her thirty days' leave was over, one of Mari's colleagues turned up at the house. He had phoned every day, but Mari either didn't answer the phone or else asked her husband to say she was busy. That afternoon, he simply stood there ringing the bell until she opened the front door.

Mari had had a quiet morning. She made some tea and they talked about the office, and he asked her when she would be coming back to work.

'Never.'

He remembered their conversation about El Salvador.

'You've always worked hard, and you have the right to choose what you want to do,' he said, with no rancour in his voice. 'But I think that, in cases such as these, work is the best therapy. Do some travelling, see the world, go wherever you think you might be useful, but the doors of the office are always open, awaiting your return.'

When she heard this, Mari burst into tears, which she often did now, with great ease.

Her colleague waited for her to calm down. Like a good lawyer, he didn't ask anything; he knew he had more chance of getting a reply to his silence than to any question.

And so it was. Mari told him the whole story, from what had happened in the cinema to her recent hysterical attacks on her husband, who had given her so much support.

'I'm mad,' she said.

'Possibly,' he replied, with an all-knowing air, but with real tenderness in his voice. 'In that case, you have two options: either get some treatment or continue being ill.'

'There isn't any treatment for what I'm feeling. I'm still in full possession of all my mental faculties and I'm worried because this situation has gone on now for such a long time. I don't haven't any of the classic symptoms of madness, like withdrawal from reality, apathy or uncontrolled aggression, just fear.'

'That's what all mad people say, that they're perfectly normal.'

The two of them laughed and she made some more tea. They talked about the weather, the success of Slovenian independence, the growing tensions between Croatia and Yugoslavia. Mari watched TV all day and was very well informed.

Before saying goodbye, her colleague touched on the subject again.

'They've just opened a new hospital in the city,' he said, 'backed by foreign money and offering first-class treatment.'

'Treatment for what?'

'Imbalances, shall we say. And excessive fear is definitely an imbalance.'

Mari promised to think about it, but she still took no real decision. She continued to have panic attacks for another month, until she realised that not only her personal life but her marriage was on the point of collapse. Again she asked for some tranquillisers and again she managed to set foot outside the house, for only the second time in sixty days.

She took a taxi and went to the new hospital. On the way, the driver asked if she was going to visit someone.

'They say it's very comfortable, but apparently they've got some real nutters in there too, and part of the treatment includes electric shocks.'

'I'm going to visit someone,' said Mari.

It took only an hour of conversation for Mari's two months of suffering to come to an end. The director of the hospital – a tall man with dyed hair, who answered to the name of Dr Igor – explained that it was merely a panic disorder, a recently recognised illness in the annals of world psychiatry.

'That doesn't mean it's a new illness,' he explained, taking care to make himself clear.

'What happens is that the people affected by it tend to hide, afraid they'll be mistaken for mad people. It's just a chemical imbalance in the body, as is depression.'

Dr Igor wrote her a prescription and told her to go back home.

'I don't want to go back now,' said Mari. 'Even after all you've told me, I won't have the courage to go out into the street. My marriage has become a hell, and my husband needs time to recover from these months he's spent looking after me.'

As always happened in such cases – because the share-holders wanted to keep the hospital working at full capacity – Dr Igor accepted her as a patient, although making it absolutely clear that it wasn't necessary.

Mari received the necessary medication, along with the appropriate psychiatric treatment, and the symptoms diminished and finally disappeared altogether.

During that time, however, the story of her internment in the hospital went the rounds of the small city of Ljubljana. Her colleague, a friend of many years, and companion of who knows how many moments of joy and trepidation, came to visit her in Villete. He complimented her on her courage in following his advice and getting help, but he then went on to explain the real reason for his visit:

'Perhaps it really is time you retired.'

Mari knew what lay behind those words: no one was going to entrust their affairs to a lawyer who had been a mental patient.

'You said that work was the best therapy. I need to come back, even if only for a short time.'

She waited for a response, but he said nothing. Mari went on:

'You were the one who suggested I get treatment. When I was considering retirement, my idea was to leave on a high note, fulfilled, having made a free, spontaneous decision. I don't want to leave my job just like that, defeated. At least give me a chance to win back my self-esteem, and then I'll ask to retire.'

The lawyer cleared his throat.

'I suggested you get treatment, I didn't say anything about going into hospital.'

'But it was a question of survival. I was too afraid to go out into the street, my marriage was falling apart.'

Mari knew she was wasting her words. Nothing she could say would persuade him; after all, it was the prestige of the office that was at risk. Even so, she tried once more.

'Inside here, I've lived with two sorts of people: those who have no chance of ever going back into society and those who are completely cured, but who prefer to pretend to be mad rather than face up to life's responsibilities. I want and need to learn to like myself again, I have to convince myself that I'm capable of taking my own decisions. I can't be pushed into decisions not of my own making.'

'We're allowed to make a lot of mistakes in our lives,' said her colleague, 'except the mistake that destroys us.'

There was no point in continuing the conversation; in his opinion, Mari had committed the fatal error.

Two days later, she received a visit from another lawyer, this time from a different practice, her now ex-colleagues' greatest rival. Mari cheered up; perhaps he knew she was free to take up a new post, and there was a chance she could regain her place in the world.

The lawyer came into the visiting room, sat down opposite her, smiled, asked if she was feeling better and then took various papers out of his briefcase.

'I'm here at your husband's request,' he said.

'This is an application for divorce. Obviously, though, he'll continue to pay all your hospital bills for as long as you remain in here.'

This time Mari did not attempt to argue. She signed everything, even though she knew that, in accordance with the law she had studied and practised, she could prolong the quarrel indefinitely. She then went straight to see Dr Igor and told him that her symptoms had returned.

Dr Igor knew she was lying, but he nevertheless extended her internment for an indefinite period.

Veronika decided she would have to go to bed, but Eduard was still standing by the piano.

'I'm tired, Eduard. I need to sleep.'

She would like to continue playing for him, dredging up from her anaesthetised memory all the sonatas, requiems and adagios she used to know, because he knew how to admire without appearing to demand anything of her. But her body could take no more.

He was so good-looking. If only he would take one step outside his world and see her as a woman, then her last nights on this earth might be the most beautiful of her entire life: Eduard was the only one capable of understanding that Veronika was an artist. Through the pure emotion of a sonata or a minuet she had forged a bond with this man such as she had never known with anyone else.

Eduard was the ideal man, sensitive, educated; a man who had destroyed an indifferent world in order to recreate it again in his head, this time with new colours, new characters, new stories. And this new world included a woman, a piano and a moon that was continuing to grow.

'I could fall in love right now and give everything I have to you,' she said, knowing that he couldn't understand her. 'All you ask from me is a little music, but I am much more than I ever thought I was, and I would like to share other things with you that I have only just begun to understand.'

Eduard smiled. Had he understood? Veronika felt afraid – all the manuals of good behaviour say that you should never speak of love so directly, and never to a man you barely know. But she decided to continue, because she had nothing to lose.

'You're the only man on the face of the Earth with whom I could fall in love, Eduard, for the simple reason that, when I die, you will not miss me. I don't know what a schizophrenic feels, but I'm sure they never miss anyone.

'Perhaps, to begin with, you'll miss the fact that there's no more night music, but the moon will still rise, there'll be someone willing to play sonatas for you, especially in a hospital, where each and every one of us is a "lunatic".'

She didn't quite know what the relationship was between mad people and the moon, but it must be a strong one, if they used a word like that to describe the mad.

'And I won't miss you either, Eduard, because I will be dead, far from here. And since I'm not afraid of losing you, I don't care what you think or don't think about me. Tonight I played for you like a woman in love. It was wonderful. It was the best moment of my entire life.'

She looked at Mari outside in the garden. She remembered her words. And again she looked at the man standing in front of her.

Veronika took off her sweater and moved closer to Eduard. If she was going to do something, let it be now. Mari would put up with the cold out there for a long time and only then would she come back in.

He stepped back. The question in his eyes was this: when was she going to play the piano again? When would she play a new piece of music to fill his soul with the same colour, pain, suffering and joy of those mad composers who had leapt the generations with their work?

'The woman outside told me to masturbate and to find out how far I could go. Could I really go farther than I've ever been before?'

She took his hand and tried to pull him towards the sofa, but Eduard politely declined. He preferred to remain standing where he was, beside the piano, waiting patiently for her to play again.

Veronika was disconcerted at first and then realised that she had nothing to lose. She was dead, what was the point of continuing to feed the fears or preconceptions that had always limited her life? She took off her blouse, her trousers, her bra, her pants, and stood before him naked.

Eduard laughed. She didn't know why, she merely noted that he had laughed. Delicately, she took his hand and placed it on her genitals; his hand remained there, immobile. Veronika gave up the idea and removed his hand.

Something was exciting her far more than any physical contact with this man: the fact that she could do whatever she wanted, that there were no limits. Apart from the woman outside, who might come back in at any moment, nobody else would be awake.

Her blood began to race, and the cold – which she had felt when she took off her clothes – was fading. Veronika and Eduard were both standing up, face to face, she naked, he fully clothed. Veronika slid her own hand down to her genitals and started to masturbate; she had done it before, either alone or with certain partners, but never in a situation like this, where the man showed no apparent interest in what was happening.

And this was exciting, very exciting. Standing up, legs apart, Veronika was touching her genitals, her breasts, her hair, surrendering herself as she had never done before, not because she wanted to see Eduard leave his distant world, but because this was something she had never experienced before.

She started talking, saying unthinkable things, things that her parents, her friends, her ancestors would have considered absolute filth. Her first orgasm came and she bit her lips so as not to cry out with pleasure.

Eduard was looking at her. There was a different light in his eyes, as if he understood, even if it was only the energy, heat, sweat and smell that her body gave off. Veronika was still not satisfied. She knelt down and started masturbating again.

She wanted to die of orgasmic pleasure, thinking about and realising everything that had always been forbidden to her: she begged him to touch her, to force her, to use her in any way he wanted. She wished Zedka was there too, because a woman knows how to touch another woman's body better than any man, because she already knows all its secrets.

On her knees before Eduard, who remained standing, she felt possessed, touched, and she used coarse words to describe what she wanted him to do to her. Another orgasm came, stronger than ever, as if everything around her were about to explode. She remembered the heart attack she had had that morning, but what did that matter, she would die in one great explosion of pleasure. She was tempted to touch Eduard – he was there before her – but she did not want to risk spoiling the moment. She was going far, very far, just as Mari had said.

She imagined herself both queen and slave, dominatrix and victim. In her imagination, she was making love with men of all skin colours – white, black, yellow – with homosexuals and beggars. She was anyone's and anyone could do anything to her. She had one, two, three orgasms one after the other. She imagined everything she had never imagined before and she gave herself to all that was most base and most pure. At last, unable to contain herself any longer, she cried out with pleasure, with the pain of all those orgasms, all those men and women who had entered and left her body through the doors of her mind.

She lay down on the ground and stayed there, drenched in sweat, her soul full of peace. She had concealed her hidden desires even from herself, unable to say why, but she needed no answer. It was enough that she had done what she had done: she had surrendered herself.

Gradually, the universe returned to its proper place and Veronika stood up. Eduard had not moved in all that time, but there seemed to be something different about him: there was a tenderness in his eyes, a very human tenderness.

'It was so good that I can see love in everything, even in the eyes of a schizophrenic.'

She was beginning to put her clothes back on, when she felt a third presence in the room.

Mari was there. Veronika didn't know when she had come in or what she had heard or seen, but even so she felt no shame or fear. She merely looked at her distantly, as one does at someone who has come too close.

'I did as you suggested,' she said. 'And I went a long, long way.'

Mari said nothing; she had just been reliving certain vital moments of her past life, and she was feeling slightly uneasy. Perhaps it was time to return to the world, to face up to things out there, to say that everyone could be a member of a great Fraternity, even if they had never been in a mental hospital.

Like this young girl, for example, whose only reason for being in Villete was because she had made an attempt on her own life. She had never known panic, depression, mystical visions, psychoses – the limits to which the mind can take us. Although she had known many men, she had never experienced the most hidden part of her own desires, and the result was that half of her life had been unknown to her. If only everyone could know and live with their inner madness. Would the world be a worse place for it? No, people would be fairer and happier.

'Why did I never do that before?'

'He wants you to play more music,' said Mari, looking at Eduard. 'I think he deserves it.'

'I will, but answer my question first: why did I never do that before? If I'm free, if I can think whatever I choose to think, why have I always avoided imagining forbidden situations?'

'Forbidden? Listen, I was a lawyer and I know the law. I was also a Catholic and I used to know whole sections of the Bible by heart. What do you mean by "forbidden"?'

Mari went over to her and helped her on with her sweater.

'Look me in the eye and never forget what I'm about to tell you. There are only two prohibitions, one according to man's law, the other according to God's. Never force a sexual relationship on anyone, because that is considered to be rape. And never have sexual relations with children, because that is the worst of all sins. Apart from that, you're free. There's always someone who wants exactly what you want.'

Mari didn't have the patience to teach important things to someone who was about to die. With a smile, she said good night and left the room.

Eduard didn't move; he was waiting for the music. Veronika needed to reward him for the immense pleasure he had given her, merely by staying with her and witnessing her madness without horror or repulsion. She sat down at the piano and started to play again.

Her soul was light, and not even the fear of death torment-
ed her now. She had experienced what she had always kept hidden from herself. She had experienced the pleasures of virgin
and prostitute, of slave and queen, albeit more slave than
queen.

That night, as if by a miracle, all the songs she had known
returned to her memory, and she played in order to give Eduard
as much pleasure as she herself had experienced.

When he turned on the light, Dr Igor was surprised to see the young woman sitting in the waiting room outside his office.

'It's still very early. And I'm completely booked up all day.'

'I know it's early,' she said. 'And the day hasn't yet begun. I just need to talk for a while, only a short while. I need your help.'

She had dark shadows under her eyes and her hair was dull, the typical symptoms of someone who has spent the whole night awake.

Dr Igor decided to show her into his room.

He asked her to sit down, while he turned on the light and opened the curtains. It would be dawn in less than an hour, and then he would be able to save on electricity; the shareholders were very hot on expenses, however insignificant.

He glanced rapidly through his diary: Zedka had had her last insulin shock and had reacted positively, that is, she had managed to survive that inhuman treatment. Just as well, in this particular case, that Dr Igor had demanded that the hospital council sign a declaration taking full responsibility for the consequences.

He started reading some reports. Two or three patients had behaved aggressively during the night, amongst them, according to the nurses' report, Eduard. He had gone back to his ward at about four in the morning and had refused to take his sleeping tablets. Dr Igor would have to act. However liberal Villete might be inside, it was necessary to preserve its image as a harsh, conservative institution.

'I've got something very important to ask you,' said Veronika.

But Dr Igor ignored her. Picking up his stethoscope, he began to listen to her heart and lungs. He tested her reflexes and examined the back of her retina with a small torch. He saw that there were now almost no signs of Vitriol poisoning, or Bitterness as some preferred to call it.

He immediately went to the phone and asked the nurse to bring in some medication with a complicated name.

'It seems you didn't have your injection last night,' he said.

'But I'm feeling much better.'

'I just have to look at your face: dark shadows under the eyes, tiredness, the lack of immediate reflexes. If you want to make the most of the little time left to you, please do as I say.'

'That's exactly why I'm here. I want to make the most of that little time, but in my own way. How much time have I actually got?'

Dr Igor peered at her over the top of his glasses.

'You can tell me,' she said. 'I'm not afraid or indifferent or anything. I want to live, but I know that's not enough, and I'm resigned to my fate.'

'What is it you want then?'

The nurse came in with the injection. Dr Igor nodded and the nurse gently rolled up the sleeve of Veronika's sweater.

'How much time have I got left?' said Veronika again, while the nurse gave her the injection.

'Twenty-four hours, perhaps less.'

She looked down, and bit her lip, but managed to maintain her composure.

'I want to ask two favours. First, that you give me some medication, an injection or whatever, so that I can stay awake and enjoy every moment that remains of my life. I'm very tired, but I don't want to sleep. I've got a lot to do, things that I always postponed for some future date, in the days when I thought life would last for ever. Things I'd lost interest in, when I started to believe that life wasn't worth living.'

'And what's the second favour?'

'I want to leave here so that I can die outside. I need to visit Ljubljana castle. It's always been there and I've never even had the curiosity to go and see it close to. I need to talk to the woman who sells chestnuts in winter and flowers in the spring. We passed each other so often, and I never once asked her how she was. And I want to go out without a jacket and walk in the snow, I want to find out what extreme cold feels like, I, who was always so well wrapped up, so afraid of catching a cold.

'In short, Dr Igor, I want to feel the rain on my face, to smile at any man I feel attracted to, to accept all the coffees men might buy for me. I want to kiss my mother, tell her I love her, weep in her lap, unashamed of showing my feelings, because they were always there even though I hid them.

'I might go into a church and look at those images that never meant anything to me and see if they say something to me now. If an interesting man invites me out to a club, I'll accept, and I'll dance all night until I drop. Then I'll go to bed with him, but not the way I used to go to bed with other men, trying to stay in control, pretending things I didn't feel. I want to give myself to one man, to the city, to life and, finally, to death.'

When Veronika had finished speaking, there was a heavy silence. Doctor and patient looked each other in the eye, absorbed, perhaps distracted by all the many possibilities that a mere twenty-four hours could offer.

'I'm going to give you some stimulants, but I don't recommend you take them,' Dr Igor said at last. 'They'll keep you awake, but they'll also take away the peace you need in order to experience everything you want to experience.'

Veronika was starting to feel ill; whenever she was given that injection, something bad always happened inside her body.

'You're looking very pale. Perhaps you'd better go to bed, and we'll talk again tomorrow.'

Once more she felt like crying, but she remained in control.

'There won't be a tomorrow, as you well know. I'm tired, Dr Igor, very tired. That's why I asked for the tablets. I spent all night awake, half-desperate, half-resigned. I could succumb to another hysterical attack of fear, as happened yesterday, but what's the point? If I've still got twenty-four hours of life left, and there are so many experiences waiting for me, I decided it would be better to put aside despair.

'Please, Dr Igor, let me live a little of the time remaining to me, because we both know that tomorrow will be too late.'

'Go and sleep,' said the doctor, 'and come back here at midday. Then we'll speak again.'

Veronika saw there was no way out.

'I'll go and sleep and then I'll come back, but could I just talk to you for a few more minutes?'

'It'll have to be a few. I'm very busy today.'

'I'll come straight to the point. Last night, for the first time, I masturbated in a completely uninhibited way. I thought all the things I'd never dared to think, I took pleasure in things that before frightened or repelled me.'

Dr Igor assumed his most professional air. He didn't know where this conversation might lead and he didn't want any problems with his superiors.

'I discovered that I'm a pervert, doctor. I want to know if that played some part in my attempted suicide. There are so many things I didn't know about myself.'

'I just have to give her an answer,' he thought. 'There's no need to call in the nurse to witness the conversation, and avoid any future law suits for sexual abuse.'

'We all want different things,' he replied. 'And our partners do too. What's wrong with that?'

'You tell me.'

'There's everything wrong with it. Because when everyone dreams, but only a few realise their dreams, that makes cowards of us all.'

'Even if those few are right?'

'The person who's right is just the person who's strongest. In this case, paradoxically, it's the cowards who are the brave ones, and they manage to impose their ideas on everyone else.'

Dr Igor didn't want to go any further.

'Now, please, go and rest a little; I have other patients to see. If you do as I say, I'll see what can be done about your second request.'

Veronika left the room. The doctor's next patient was Zedka, who was due to be discharged, but Dr Igor asked her to wait a little; he needed to take a few notes on the conversation he had just had.

In his dissertation about Vitriol, he would have to include a long chapter on sex. After all, so many neuroses and psychoses had their origins in sex. He believed that fantasies were electrical impulses from the brain, which, if not realised, released their energy into other areas.

During his medical studies, Dr Igor had read an interesting treatise on sexual dissidence: sadism, masochism, homosexuality, coprophagy, coprolalia, voyeurism, the list was endless. At first, he considered these things examples of deviant behaviour in a few maladjusted people incapable of having a healthy relationship with their partners.

However, as he advanced in his profession as psychiatrist and talked to his patients, he realised that everyone has an unusual story to tell. His patients would sit down in the comfortable armchair in his office, stare hard at the floor, and begin a long dissertation on what they called 'illnesses' (as if he were not the doctor) or perversions (as if he were not the psychiatrist charged with deciding what was and wasn't perverse).

And one by one, these normal people would describe fantasies that were all to be found in that famous treatise on erotic minorities, a book, in fact, that defended the right of everyone to have the orgasm they chose, as long as it did not violate the rights of their partner.

Women who had studied in convent schools dreamed of being sexually humiliated; men in suits and ties, high-ranking civil servants, told him of the fortunes they spent on Rumanian prostitutes just so that they could lick their feet. Boys in love with boys, girls in love with their fellow schoolgirls. Husbands who wanted to watch their wives having sex with strangers, women who masturbated every time they found some hint that their men had committed adultery. Mothers who had to suppress an impulse to give themselves to the first delivery man who rang the doorbell, fathers who recounted secret adventures with the bizarre transvestites who managed to slip through the strict border controls.

And orgies. It seemed that everyone, at least once in their life, wanted to take part in an orgy.

Dr Igor put down his pen for a moment and thought about himself: what about him? Yes, he would like it too. An orgy, as he imagined it, must be something completely anarchic and joyful, in which the feeling of possession no longer existed, just pleasure and confusion.

Was that one of the main reasons why there were so many people poisoned by bitterness? Marriages restricted to an enforced monotheism, within which, according to studies that Dr Igor kept safely in his medical library, sexual desire disappeared in the third or fourth year of living together. After that, the wife felt rejected and the man felt trapped, and Vitriol, or bitterness, began to eat away at everything.

People talked more openly to a psychiatrist than they did to a priest because a doctor couldn't threaten them with Hell. During his long career as a psychiatrist, Dr Igor had heard almost everything they had to tell him.

To *tell* him, for they rarely *did* anything. Even after several years in the profession, he still asked himself why they were so afraid of being different.

When he tried to find out the reason, the most common responses were: 'My husband would think I was behaving like a prostitute', or, when it was a man: 'My wife deserves my respect.'

The conversation usually stopped there. There was no point saying that everyone has a different sexual profile, as individual as their fingerprints, no one wanted to believe that. It was very dangerous being uninhibited in bed; there was always the fear that the other person might still be a slave to their preconceived ideas.

'I'm not going to change the world,' he said, resignedly, asking the nurse to send in the ex-depressive, Zedka, 'but at least I can say what I think in my thesis.'

Eduard saw Veronika leaving Dr Igor's consulting room and making her way to the ward. He felt like telling her his secrets, opening his heart to her, with the same honesty and freedom with which, the previous night, she had opened her body to him.

It had been one of the severest tests he had been through since he had come to Villete as a schizophrenic. But he had managed to resist, and he was pleased, although his desire to return to the world was beginning to unsettle him.

'Everyone knows this young girl isn't going to last until the end of the week. There'd be no point.'

Or perhaps, precisely because of that, it would be good to share his story with her. For three years, he had spoken only to Mari, and even then he wasn't sure she had entirely understood him; as a mother, she was bound to think his parents were right, that they had just wanted the best for him, that his visions of Paradise were the foolish dreams of an adolescent completely out of touch with the real world.

Visions of Paradise. That was exactly what had led him down into hell, into endless arguments with his family, into such a powerful feeling of guilt that he had felt incapable of doing anything and had finally sought refuge in another world. If it hadn't been for Mari, he would still be living in that separate reality.

Then Mari had appeared; she had taken care of him and made him feel loved again. Thanks to her, Eduard was still capable of knowing what was going on around him.

A few days ago, a young woman the same age as him had sat down at the piano to play the *Moonlight Sonata*. Eduard had once more felt troubled by his visions of Paradise and he couldn't have said if it was the fault of the music or the young woman or the moon or the long time he had spent in Villete.

He followed her as far as the women's ward, to find his way barred by a nurse.

'You can't come in here, Eduard. Go into the garden, it's nearly dawn and it's going to be a lovely day.'

Veronika looked back.

'I'm going to sleep for a bit,' she said gently. 'We'll talk when I wake up.'

Veronika didn't know why, but that young man had become part of her world, or the little that remained of it. She was certain that Eduard was capable of understanding her music, of admiring her talent; even if he couldn't utter a word, his eyes said everything, as they did at that moment, at the door of the ward, speaking of things she didn't want to hear about.

Tenderness. Love.

'Living with mental patients is fast making me mad. Schizophrenics don't feel things like that, not for other human beings.'

Veronika felt like turning back and giving him a kiss, but she didn't; the nurse would see and tell Dr Igor, and the doctor would certainly not allow a woman who kissed schizophrenics to leave Villete.

Eduard looked at the nurse. His attraction for the young girl was stronger than he had thought, but he had to control himself. He would go and ask Mari's advice, she was the only person with whom he shared his secrets. She would doubtless tell him what he wanted to hear, that in such a case, love was both dangerous and pointless. Mari would ask Eduard to stop being so foolish and to go back to being a normal schizophrenic (and then she would giggle gleefully at her own nonsensical words).

He joined the other inmates in the refectory, ate what he was given and went outside for the obligatory walk in the garden. While 'taking the sun' (on that day the temperature was below zero), he tried to approach Mari, but she looked as if she wanted to be left alone. She didn't need to say anything, Eduard knew enough about solitude to respect other people's needs.

A new inmate came over to Eduard. He obviously didn't know anyone yet.

'God punished humanity,' he said. 'He punished it with the plague. However, I saw Him in my dreams and He asked me to come and save Slovenia.'

Eduard started to move away, while the man continued shouting:

'Do you think I'm mad? Then read the gospels. God sent His only Son and His Son has risen again.'

But Edward couldn't hear him any more. He was looking at the mountains beyond and wondering what was happening to him. Why did he feel like leaving there if he had finally found the peace he had so longed for? Why risk shaming his parents again, just when all the family problems were resolved? He began to feel agitated, pacing up and down, waiting for Mari to emerge from her silence so that they could talk, but she seemed as remote as ever.

He knew how to escape from Villete. However strict the security might seem, it was actually full of holes, simply because, once people entered Villete, they felt little desire to leave. On the west side, there was a wall that could quite easily be scaled since it was full of footholds; anyone who wanted to climb it would soon find themselves out in the countryside and, five minutes later, on a road heading north to Croatia. The war was over, brothers were once more brothers, the frontiers were no longer guarded as they had been before; with a little luck, he could be in Belgrade in six hours.

Eduard had already been on that road several times, but he had always decided to go back, because he had still not received the signal to go forward. Now things were different: the signal had finally come in the form of a young woman with green eyes, brown hair and the startled look of someone who thinks they know what they want.

Eduard thought of climbing the wall there and then, of leaving and never being seen in Slovenia again. But the girl was sleeping and he needed at least to say goodbye to her.

When everyone had finished 'taking the sun' and the Fraternity had gathered in the lounge, Eduard joined them.

'What's that madman doing here?' asked the oldest member of the group.

'Leave him alone,' said Mari. 'Anyway, we're mad too.'

They all laughed and started talking about the previous day's lecture. The question was this, could Sufi meditation really change the world? Theories were put forward, as were suggestions, methodologies, contrary ideas, criticisms of the lecturer, ways of improving what had been tested over many centuries.

Eduard was sick of this kind of discussion. These people locked themselves up in a mental hospital and set about saving the world without actually taking any risks because they knew that, outside, they would be thought ridiculous, even if some of their ideas were very practical. Everyone had their own theory about everything, and they believed that their truth was the only one that mattered. They spent days, nights, weeks and years talking, never accepting the fact that, good or bad, an idea only exists when someone tries to put it into practice.

What was Sufi meditation? What was God? What was salvation if, that is, the world needed saving? Nothing. If everyone there – and outside Villete too – just lived their lives and let others do the same, God would be in every moment, in every grain of mustard, in the fragment of cloud that is there and then gone the following moment. God was there and yet people believed they still had to go on looking, because it seemed too simple to accept that life was an act of faith.

He remembered the exercise he had heard the Sufi master teaching while he was waiting for Veronika to come back to the piano: simply look at a rose. What more was necessary?

Yet even after the experience of that deep meditation, even after having been brought so close to a vision of Paradise, there they were, discussing, arguing, criticising and constructing theories.

His eyes met Mari's. She looked away, but Eduard was determined to put an end to that situation once and for all; he went over to her and took her by the arm.

'Stop it, Eduard.'

He could say: 'Come with me.' But he didn't want to do so in front of all those people, who would be surprised at his forthright tone. That's why he preferred to kneel down and look beseechingly up at her.

The men and women laughed.

'You've become a saint for him, Mari,' someone said. 'It must have been yesterday's meditation.'

But Eduard's years of silence had taught him to speak with his eyes; he was able to pour all his energies into them. Just as he was absolutely sure that Veronika had understood his tenderness and love, he knew that Mari would understand his despair, because he really needed her.

She resisted a little longer, then she got up and took him by the hand.

'Let's go for a walk,' she said. 'You're upset.'

They went out into the garden again. As soon as they were at a safe distance, certain that no one could hear them, Eduard broke the silence.

'I've been in Villete for years,' he said. 'I've stopped being an embarrassment to my parents, I've set aside all my ambitions, but still the visions of Paradise remain.'

'I know,' said Mari. 'We've often talked about it, and I know what you're leading up to as well: it's time to leave.'

Eduard glanced up at the sky; did Mari feel the same?

'And it's because of the girl,' said Mari. 'We've seen a lot of people die here, always when they least expected it, and usually after they'd entirely given up on life. But this is the first time we've seen it happening to a young, pretty, healthy person with so much to live for. Veronika is the only one who doesn't want to stay in Villete for ever. And that makes us ask ourselves: What about us? What are we doing here?'

He nodded.

'Then, last night, I too asked myself what I was doing in this hospital. And I thought how very interesting to be down in the square, at the Three Bridges, in the market place opposite the theatre, buying apples and talking about the weather. Obviously, I'd be struggling with a lot of other long-forgotten things, like unpaid bills, problems with neighbours, the ironic looks of people who don't understand me, solitude, my children's carping. But all that is just part of life, I think; and the price you pay for having to deal with those minor problems is far less than the price you pay for not recognising they're yours. I'm thinking of going round to my ex-husband's tonight, just to say "Thank you". What do you think?'

'I don't know. Do you think I should go to my parents' house too and say the same thing?'

'Possibly. Basically, everything that happens in our life is our fault and ours alone. A lot of people go through the same difficulties we went through, and they react completely differently. We looked for the easiest way out: a separate reality.'

Eduard knew that Mari was right.

'I feel like starting to live again, Eduard. I feel like making the mistakes I always wanted to make, but never had the courage to, facing up to the feelings of panic that might well come back, but whose presence will merely weary me, since I know I'm not going to die or faint because of them. I can make new friends and teach them how to be mad too in order to be wise. I'll tell them not to follow the manual of good behaviour but to discover their own lives, desires, adventures and to LIVE. I'll quote from Ecclesiastes to the Catholics, from the Koran to the Muslims, from the Torah to the Jews, from Aristotle to the atheists. I never want to be a lawyer again, but I can use my experience to give lectures about men and women who knew the truth about this existence of ours and whose writings can be summed up in one word: Live. If you live, God will live with you. If you refuse to run his risks, He'll retreat to that distant Heaven and be merely a subject for philosophical speculation. Everyone knows this, but no one takes the first step, perhaps for fear of being called mad. At least, we haven't got that fear, Eduard. We've already been inmates of Villete.'

'The only thing we can't do is stand as candidates for President of the Republic. The opposition would be sure to probe into our past.'

Mari laughed and agreed.

'I'm tired of the life here. I don't know if I'll manage to

overcome my fear, but I've had enough of the Fraternity, of this garden, of Villete, of pretending to be mad.'

'If I do it, will you?'

'You won't do it.'

'I almost did, just a few moments ago.'

'I don't know. I'm tired of all this, but I'm used to it too.'

'When I came here, diagnosed as a schizophrenic, you spent days, months, talking to me and treating me as a human being. I was getting used to the life I'd decided to lead, to the other reality I'd created, but you wouldn't let me. I hated you and now I love you. I want you to leave Villete, Mari, just as I left my separate universe.'

Mari moved off without answering.

In the small and never used library in Villete, Eduard didn't find the Koran or Aristotle or any of the other philosophers that Mari had mentioned. He found instead the words of a poet:

Then I said in my heart, As it happeneth to the fool
so will it happen even to me...
Go thy way, eat thy bread with joy,
and drink thy wine with a merry heart;
for God hath already accepted thy works.
Let thy garments be always white;
and let not thy head lack ointment.
Live joyfully with the wife whom thou lovest
all the days of the life of thy vanity,
which he hath given thee under the sun,
all the days of thy vanity:
for that is thy portion in life,
and in thy labour wherein thou labourest under the sun...

139

Walk in the ways of thine heart,
and in the sight of thine eyes:
but know thou, that for all these things
God will bring thee into judgement.

'God will bring me into judgement,' said Eduard out loud, 'and I will say: "For a time in my life I stood looking at the wind, I forgot to sow, I did not live joyfully, I did not even drink the wine offered me. But one day, I judged myself ready, and I went back to work. I told men about my visions of Paradise, as did Bosch, Van Gogh, Wagner, Beethoven, Einstein and other madmen before me." Fine, let Him say that I left hospital in order to avoid seeing a young girl dying; she will be there in Heaven, and she will intercede for me.'

'What are you saying?' said the man in charge of the library.

'I want to leave Villete,' said Eduard, in a slightly louder voice than normal. 'I've got things to do.'

The librarian rang a bell, and a few moments later, two nurses appeared.

'I want to leave,' said Eduard again, agitated. 'I'm fine, just let me talk to Dr Igor.'

But the two men already had hold of him, one on each arm. Eduard tried to free himself from the arms of the nurses, though he knew it was useless.

'You're having a bit of a crisis, now just keep calm,' said one of them. 'We'll take care of it.'

Eduard started to struggle.

'Let me talk to Dr Igor. I've got a lot to tell him, I'm sure he'll understand.'

The men were already dragging him towards the ward.

'Let me go,' he was yelling. 'Just let me talk for a minute.'

The way to the ward was through the lounge, and all the other inmates were gathered there. Eduard was struggling and things were starting to look ugly.

'Let him go! He's mad!'

Some laughed, others beat with their hands on chairs and tables.

'This is a mental hospital. No one here is obliged to behave the way you do.'

One of the nurses whispered to the other:

'We'd better give them a fright, otherwise the situation will get completely out of control.'

'There's only one way.'

'Dr Igor won't like it.'

'He'll like it still less if this gang of maniacs start smashing up his beloved hospital.'

Veronika woke up with a start, in a cold sweat. There was a terrible noise outside, and she needed silence to go on sleeping. But the racket continued.

Feeling slightly dizzy, she got out of bed and went into the lounge, just in time to see Eduard being dragged off, while other nurses were rushing in, wielding syringes.

'What are you doing?' she screamed.

'Veronika!'

The schizophrenic had spoken to her. He had said her name. With a mixture of surprise and shame, she tried to approach, but one of the nurses stopped her.

'What are you doing? I'm not here because I'm mad. You can't treat me like this.'

She managed to push the nurse away, while the other inmates continued to shout and kick up what seemed to her a terrifying din. Should she go and find Dr Igor and leave there at once?

'Veronika!'

He had said her name again. Making a superhuman effort, Eduard managed to break free from the two male nurses. Instead of running away, though, he stood there, motionless, just as he had the previous night. As if transfixed by a conjuring trick, everyone stopped, waiting for the next move.

One of the nurses came over again, but Eduard looked at him, summoning all his strength.

'I'll go with you, I know where you're taking me, and I know too that you want everyone else to know. Just wait a minute.'

The nurse decided it was worth taking the risk; after all, everything seemed to have returned to normal.

'I think...I think you're important to me,' said Eduard to Veronika.

'You can't speak. You don't live in this world, you don't know that my name's Veronika. You weren't with me last night, please, say you weren't there.'

'I was.'

She took his hand. The mad people were shouting, applauding, making obscene remarks.

'Where are they taking you?'

'For some treatment.'

'I'll come with you.'

'It's not worth it. You'd just be frightened, even if I swear to you that it doesn't hurt, that you don't feel anything. And it's much better than sedatives because you recover your lucidity much more quickly.'

Veronika didn't know what he was talking about. She regretted having taken his hand, she wanted to get away from there as soon as possible, to hide her shame, never again to see that man who had witnessed all that was most sordid in her, and who nevertheless continued to treat her with such tenderness.

But again, she remembered Mari's words: she didn't need to explain her life to anyone, not even to that young man standing before her.

'I'll come with you.'

The nurses thought it might be better like that. The schizophrenic no longer needed to be restrained, he was going of his own free will.

When they reached the ward, Eduard lay down on the bed. There were two other men waiting, with a strange machine and a bag containing strips of cloth.

Eduard turned to Veronika and asked her to sit down on the bed.

'In a few minutes, the story will be all round Villete and people will calm down again, because even the maddest of the mad feel fear. Only someone who has experienced this knows that it isn't as terrible as it seems.'

The nurses listened to the conversation and didn't believe a word of what the schizophrenic was saying. It must hurt terribly, but then who knows what goes on inside the head of a madman? The only sensible thing the young man had said was about fear: the story *would* soon be all round Villete and calm would swiftly be restored.

'You lay down too soon,' said one of them.

Eduard got up again, and they spread a kind of rubber sheet beneath him.

'Now you can lie down.'

He obeyed. He was perfectly calm, as if everything that was happening was absolutely routine.

The nurses tied some of the strips of cloth round Eduard's body and placed a piece of rubber in his mouth.

'It's so that he doesn't accidentally bite his tongue,' said one of the men to Veronika, pleased to be able to give some technical information as well as a warning.

They placed the strange machine – not much larger than a shoe box, with a few buttons and three dials on it – on a chair by the bed. Two wires came out of the top part and were connected to what looked like earphones.

One of the nurses placed these 'earphones' on Eduard's temples. The other seemed to be regulating the machine, twiddling some knobs, now to the right, now to the left. Although he couldn't speak because of the piece of rubber in his mouth, Eduard kept his eyes fixed on hers, and seemed to be saying: 'Don't worry, don't be afraid.'

'It's set at 130 volts for 0.3 seconds,' said the nurse controlling the machine. 'Here goes.'

He pressed a button and the machine buzzed. At that moment, Eduard's eyes glazed over, his body thrashed about on the bed with such fury that, but for the straps holding him down, he would have broken his spine.

'Stop it!' shouted Veronika.

'We have,' said the nurse, removing the 'headphones' from Eduard's temples. Even so, Eduard's body continued to writhe about, his head rocking from side to side, so violently that one of the men had to hold it still. The other nurse put the machine in a bag and sat down to smoke a cigarette.

The scene lasted a matter of moments. Eduard's body seemed to return to normal, but then the spasms recommenced, and the nurse had to redouble his efforts to keep Eduard's head still. After a while, the contractions lessened, until they stopped altogether. Eduard's eyes were wide open, and one of the nurses closed them, as one does with the dead.

Then he removed the piece of rubber from Eduard's mouth, untied him and put the strips of cloth in the bag along with the machine.

'The effects of electric shock treatment last about an hour,' he said to the girl, who was no longer shouting and who seemed mesmerised by what she was seeing. 'It's all right, he'll soon be back to normal and he'll be calmer too.'

As soon as the electric charge took effect, Eduard felt what he had experienced before: his normal vision gradually decreased, as if someone were closing a curtain, until everything disappeared. There was no pain or suffering, but he had seen other people being treated with electric shock and he knew how awful it looked.

Eduard was at peace now. If, moments before, he had experienced the stirrings of a new emotion in his heart, if he had begun to understand that love was something other than what his parents gave him, the electric shock treatment – or electroconvulsive therapy (ECT) as the specialists preferred to call it – would certainly restore him to normality.

The main effect of ECT was to destroy short-term memory. There would be no nurturing of impossible dreams for Eduard. He could not continue looking forward to a future that did not exist; his thoughts must remain turned toward the past, or he would again begin wanting to return to life.

An hour later, Zedka went into the ward, almost deserted apart from a bed, where a young man was lying, and a chair, where a young woman was sitting.

When she got closer, she saw that the young woman had been sick again, and that her bent head was lolling slightly to the right.

Zedka turned to call for help, but Veronika looked up.

'It's all right,' she said. 'I had another attack, but it's over now.'

Zedka gently helped her up and led her to the toilet.

'It's a men's toilet,' Veronika said.

'Don't worry, there's no one here.'

She removed Veronika's filthy sweater, washed it and placed it on the radiator. Then, she removed her own woollen top, and gave it to Veronika.

'Keep it. I only came to say goodbye.'

The girl seemed distant, as if she had lost all interest in life. Zedka led her back to the chair where she had been sitting.

'Eduard will wake up soon. He may have difficulty remembering what happened, but his memory will soon come back. Don't be frightened if he doesn't recognise you at first.'

'I won't be,' said Veronika, 'because I don't even recognise myself.'

Zedka pulled up a chair and sat down beside her. She had been in Villete so long, it would cost her nothing to spend a few minutes longer keeping Veronika company.

'Do you remember when we first met? I told you a story to try to explain that the world is exactly as we see it. Everyone thought the king was mad, because he wanted to impose an order that no longer existed in the minds of his subjects.

'There are things in life, though, which, however we look at them, are valid for everyone. Like love, for example.'

Zedka noticed a change in Veronika's eyes. She decided to go on.

'I would say that if someone only has a short time to live and decides to spend that time sitting beside a bed, watching a man sleeping, then that must be love. I'd go further: if, during that time, that person has a heart attack, but sits on in silence, just so as to remain close to the man, I would say that such love had a lot of potential for growth.'

'It might also be despair,' said Veronika. 'An attempt to prove that, after all, there are no reasons to continue battling away beneath the sun. I can't be in love with a man who lives in another world.'

'We all live in our own world. But if you look up at the starry sky, you'll see that all the different worlds up there combine to form constellations, solar systems, galaxies.'

Veronika got up and went over to Eduard. Tenderly, she smoothed his hair. She was glad to have someone to talk to.

'A long time ago, when I was just a child, and my mother was forcing me to learn the piano, I said to myself that I would only be able to play it well when I was in love. Last night, for the first time in my life, I felt the notes leaving my fingers as if I had no control over what I was doing.

'A force was guiding me, constructing melodies and chords that I never even knew I could play. I gave myself to the piano because I had just given myself to this man, without him even touching a hair of my head. I was not myself yesterday, not when I gave myself over to sex or when I played the piano. And yet I think I *was* myself.' Veronika shook her head.'Nothing of what I'm saying makes any sense.'

Zedka remembered her encounters in space with all those beings floating in different dimensions. She wanted to tell Veronika about it, but was afraid she might just confuse her even more.

'Before you say again that you're going to die, I want to tell you something. There are people who spend their entire lives searching for a moment like the one you had last night, but they never achieve it. That's why, if you were to die now, you would die with your heart full of love.'

Zedka got up.

'You've got nothing to lose. Many people don't allow themselves to love, precisely because of that, because there are a lot of things at risk, a lot of future and a lot of past. In your case, there is only the present.'

She went over and gave Veronika a kiss.

'If I stay here any longer, I won't leave at all. I'm cured of my depression, but in Villete, I've learned that there are other kinds of madness. I want to carry those with me and begin to see life with my own eyes.

'When I came here, I was deeply depressed. Now I'm proud to say I'm mad. Outside, I'll behave exactly like everyone else. I'll go shopping at the supermarket, I'll exchange trivialities with my friends, I'll waste precious time watching television. But I know that my soul is free and that I can dream and talk with other worlds which, before I came here, I didn't even imagine existed.

'I'm going to allow myself to do a few foolish things, just so that people can say: she's just been released from Villete. But I know that my soul is complete, because my life has meaning. I'll be able to look at a sunset and believe that God is behind it. When someone irritates me, I'll tell them what I think of them, and I won't worry what they think of me, because everyone will say: she's just been released from Villete.

'I'll look at men in the street, right in their eyes, and I won't feel guilty about feeling desired. But immediately after that, I'll go into a shop selling imported goods, buy the best wines my money can buy and I'll drink that wine with the husband I adore, because I want to laugh with him again.

'And laughing, he'll say: "You're mad!" And I'll say: "Of course I am, I was in Villete, remember! And madness freed me. Now, my dear husband, you must have a holiday every year, and make me climb some dangerous mountains, because I need to run the risk of being alive."

'People will say: "She's just been released from Villete and now she's making her husband mad too." And he will realise they're right and he'll thank God because our marriage is starting all over again and because we're both mad, like those who first invented love.'

Zedka left the ward, humming a tune Veronika had never heard before.

The day had proved exhausting, but rewarding. Dr Igor was trying to maintain the *sangfroid* and indifference of a scientist, but he could barely control his enthusiasm. The tests he was carrying out to find a cure for Vitriol poisoning were yielding surprising results.

'You haven't got an appointment today,' he said to Mari, who had come in without knocking.

'It won't take long. I'd just like to ask your opinion about something.'

'Today everyone just wants to ask my opinion,' thought Dr Igor, remembering the young girl's question about sex.

'Eduard has just been given electric shock treatment.'

'Electroconvulsive therapy, please use the correct name, otherwise it will look as if we're a mere band of barbarians.' Dr Igor tried to hide his surprise, but later, he would go and find out who had taken that decision. 'And if you want my opinion on the subject, I must make it clear that ECT is not used today as it used to be.'

'But it's dangerous.'

'It used to be *very* dangerous; they didn't know the exact voltage to use, where precisely to place the electrodes, and a lot of people died of brain haemorrhages during treatment. But things have changed: nowadays, ECT is being used with far greater technical precision and it has the advantage of provoking immediate amnesia, avoiding the chemical poisoning that comes with prolonged use of drugs. Read the psychiatric journals and don't confuse ECT with the electric shock treatment used by South American torturers. Right, you've heard my opinion. Now I must get back to my work.'

Mari didn't move.

'That isn't what I came to ask. I want to know if I can leave.'

'You can leave whenever you want and come back whenever you want, because your husband has enough money to keep you in an expensive place like this. Perhaps you should ask me: am I cured? And my reply will be another question: cured of what? You'll say: cured of my fear, of my panic attacks. And I'll say, well, Mari, you haven't actually suffered from that for the last three years.'

'So I'm cured.'

'Of course not. That wasn't what your illness was about. In the thesis I'm writing for the Slovenian Academy of Sciences' (Dr Igor didn't want to go into any detail about Vitriol), 'I'm trying to study so-called normal human behaviour. A lot of doctors before me have made similar studies and reached the conclusion that normality is merely a matter of consensus, that is, a lot of people think something is right, and so that thing becomes right.

'Some things are governed by common sense: putting buttons on the front of a shirt is a matter of logic, since it would be very difficult to button them up at the side, and impossible if they were at the back.

'Other things, however, become fixed because more and more people believe that's the way they should be. I'll give you two examples. Have you ever wondered why the keys on a typewriter are arranged in that particular order?'

'No, I haven't.'

'We call it the QWERTY keyboard, because that's the order of the letters on the first row of keys. I once wondered why it was like that and I found the answer: the first machine was invented by Christopher Scholes, in 1873, to improve calligraphy, but there was a problem: if a person typed very fast, the keys got stuck together and stopped the machine working. Then Scholes designed the QWERTY keyboard, *a keyboard that would oblige typists to type more slowly.*'

'I don't believe it.'

'But it's true. It so happened that Remington – who were sewing machine manufacturers at the time – used the QWERTY keyboard for their first typewriters. That meant that more people were forced to learn that particular system, and more companies started to make those keyboards, until it became the only available model. To repeat: the keyboard on typewriters and computers was designed so that people would type more slowly, not more quickly, do you understand? If you changed the letters around, you wouldn't find anyone to buy your product.'

When she saw a keyboard for the first time, Mari had wondered why the letters weren't in alphabetical order, but she had then promptly forgotten about it. She assumed it was simply the best layout in order for people to type quickly.

'Have you ever been to Florence?' asked Dr Igor.

'No.'

'You should go there, it's not far, for that is where you will find my second example. In the cathedral in Florence, there's a beautiful clock designed by Paolo Uccello in 1443. Now the curious thing about this clock is that, although it keeps time like all other clocks, its hands go in the opposite direction to that of normal clocks.'

'What's that got to do with my illness?'

'I'm just coming to that. When he made this clock, Paolo Uccello was not trying to be original: the fact is that, at the time, there were clocks like his as well as others with hands that went in the direction we're familiar with now. For some unknown reason, perhaps because the Duke had a clock with hands that went in the direction we now think of as the 'right' direction, that became the only direction, and Uccello's clock then seemed an aberration, a madness.'

Dr Igor paused, but he knew that Mari was following his reasoning.

'So, let's turn to your illness: each human being is unique, each with their own qualities, instincts, forms of pleasure and desire for adventure. However, society always imposes on us a collective way of behaving, and people never stop to wonder why they should behave like that. They just accept it, the way typists accepted the fact that the QWERTY keyboard was the best possible one. Have you ever met anyone in your entire life who asked why the hands of a clock should go in one particular direction and not in the other?'

'No.'

'If someone were to ask, the response they got would probably be: "You're mad." If they persisted, people would try to come up with a reason, but they'd soon change the subject, because there isn't a reason apart from the one I've just given you. So to go back to your question. What was it again?'

'Am I cured?'

'No. You're someone who is different, but who wants to be the same as everyone else. And that, in my view, is a serious illness.'

'Is wanting to be different a serious illness?'

'It is if you force yourself to be the same as everyone else: it causes neuroses, psychoses and paranoia. It's a distortion of nature, it goes against God's laws, for in all the world's woods and forests, He did not create a single leaf the same as another. But you think it's mad to be different and that's why you chose to live in Villete, because everyone is different here, and so you appear to be the same as everyone else. Do you understand?'

Mari nodded.

'People go against nature because they lack the courage to be different, and then the organism starts to produce Vitriol, or Bitterness as this poison is more commonly known.'

'What's Vitriol?'

Dr Igor realised he had gone too far and decided to change the subject.

'That doesn't matter. What I mean is this: everything indicates that you are not cured.'

Mari had years of experience in law courts and she decided to put it into practice right there and then. Her first tactic was to pretend to be in agreement with her adversary, only to draw him immediately into another line of argument.

'I agree. My reason for coming here was very concrete: I was getting panic attacks. My reason for staying was very abstract: I couldn't face the idea of a different way of life, with no job and no husband. I agree with you that I had lost the will to start a new life, a life I would have to get used to all over again. I'll go further: I agree that in a mental hospital, even with its electric shocks – sorry, ECT, as you prefer to call it – rigid timetables and occasional hysterical outbursts on the part of some inmates, the rules are easier to accept than the rules of a world which, as you say, does everything it can to conform.

'Then last night, I heard a woman playing the piano. She played superbly, in a way I've rarely heard before. As I was listening to the music, I thought of all those who had suffered in order to compose those sonatas, preludes, adagios, how foolish they must have been made to feel when they played their pieces – which were, after all, different – to those who held sway in the world of music then. I thought about the difficulties and humiliations involved in getting someone to fund an orchestra.

I thought of the booing public who were not yet used to such harmonies.

'Worse than the composers' suffering, though, was the fact that the girl was playing the music with such soul because she knew she was going to die. And am I not going to die? Where is my soul that I might play the music of my own life with such enthusiasm?'

Dr Igor was listening in silence. It seemed that all his ideas were beginning to bear fruit, but it was still too early to be sure.

'Where is my soul?' Mari asked again. 'In my past. In what I wanted my life to be. I left my soul captive in that moment when I still had a house, a husband, a job I wanted to leave but never had the courage to.

'My soul was in my past. But today it's here, I can feel it again in my body, vibrant with enthusiasm. I don't know what to do. I only know that it's taken me three years to understand that life was pushing me in a direction I didn't want to go in.'

'I think I can see some signs of improvement,' said Dr Igor.

'I don't need to ask if I can leave Villete. I can just walk through the door and never come back. But I needed to say all this to someone, and I'm saying it to you: the death of that young girl made me understand my own life.'

'I think these signs of improvement are turning into something of a miracle cure,' laughed Dr Igor. 'What do you think you'll do?'

'I'll go to El Salvador and work with children there.'

'There's no need to go so far away: Sarajevo is only about two hundred kilometres from here. The war may be over, but the problems continue.'

'Then I'll go to Sarajevo.'

Dr Igor took a form from a drawer and carefully filled it in. Then he got up and accompanied Mari to the door.

'Good luck,' he said, then immediately went back to his office and closed the door. He tried hard not to grow fond of his patients, but he never succeeded. Mari would be much missed in Villete.

When Eduard opened his eyes, the girl was still there. After his first electric shock sessions, he had had to struggle for a long time to remember what had happened; but then the therapeutic effect of the treatment lay precisely in that artificially induced partial amnesia which allowed the patient to forget the problems troubling him and to regain his calm.

However, the more frequently electric shock treatment was given, the less enduring its effects; he recognised the girl at once.

'While you were sleeping, you said something about visions of Paradise,' she said, stroking his hair.

Visions of Paradise? Yes, visions of Paradise. Eduard looked at her. He wanted to tell her everything.

At that moment, however, the nurse came in with a syringe.

'You've got to have this now,' she said to Veronika. 'Dr Igor's orders.'

'I've already had some today and I don't want any more,' she said. 'What's more I've no desire to leave here either. I refuse to obey any orders, any rules and I won't be forced to do anything.'

The nurse seemed used to this kind of reaction.

'Then, I'm afraid, we'll have to sedate you.'

'I need to talk to you,' said Eduard. 'Have the injection.'

Veronika rolled up the sleeve of her sweater, and the nurse injected her with the drug.

'There's a good girl,' she said. 'Now why don't the two of you leave this gloomy ward and go outside for a walk?'

'You're ashamed of what happened last night,' said Eduard, while they were walking in the garden.

'I was, but now I'm proud. I want to know about these visions of Paradise, because I came very close to having one myself.'

'I need to look further, beyond the buildings of Villete,' he said.

'Go on, then.'

Eduard looked behind him, not at the walls of the wards or at the garden where the inmates were walking in silence, but at a street in another continent, in a land where it either rained in torrents or not at all.

Eduard could smell that land. It was the dry season; he could feel the dust in his nostrils and the feeling gave him pleasure, because to smell the earth is to feel alive. He was riding an imported bicycle, he was seventeen, and had just left the American college in Brasília, where all the other diplomats' children studied.

He hated Brasília, but he loved the Brazilians. His father had been appointed Yugoslavian ambassador two years before, at a time when no one even dreamed of the violent division of their country. Milošević was still in power; men and women lived with their differences and tried to find a harmony beyond regional conflicts.

His father's first posting was to Brazil. Eduard dreamed of beaches, carnival, football matches and music, but they ended up in the Brazilian capital, far from the coast – a city created to provide shelter only to politicians, bureaucrats, diplomats and to their children, who didn't quite know what to do, stuck in the middle of all that.

Eduard hated living there. He spent the day immersed in his studies, trying – but failing – to relate to his classmates, trying – but failing – to work up some interest in cars, the latest trainers and designer clothes, the only possible topics of conversation with the other young people.

Now and then, there would be a party, where the boys would get drunk on one side of the room, and the girls would feign indifference on the other. There were always drugs around, and Eduard had already experimented with almost all the possible varieties, not that he could get very excited about any of them; he either got too agitated or too sleepy and immediately lost interest in what was going on around him.

His family were concerned. They had to prepare him to follow in his father's footsteps, and although Eduard had almost all the necessary talents, a desire to study, good artistic taste, a facility with languages, an interest in politics, he lacked one essential quality for a diplomat. He found it difficult to talk to other people.

His parents took him to parties, told him to invite his schoolfriends home and gave him a generous allowance, but Eduard rarely turned up with anyone. One day, his mother asked him why he didn't bring his friends to lunch or supper.

'I know every make of trainer and I know the names of all the girls who are easy to get into bed. After that, there's nothing left to talk to them about.'

Then the Brazilian girl appeared on the scene. The ambassador and his wife felt better when their son began going out on dates and coming home late. No one knew exactly where she had come from, but one night, Eduard invited her home to supper. She was a well-brought-up girl, and his parents felt contented; the boy had finally started to develop his talent for relating to other people. Moreover, they both thought – though neither actually said anything – that the girl's existence removed one great worry from their minds: Eduard clearly wasn't homosexual.

They treated Maria (that was her name) with all the consideration of future in-laws, even though they knew that in two years' time they would be transferred to another post, and they had not the slightest intention of letting their son marry someone from an exotic country. They had plans for him to meet a girl from a good family in France or Germany, who could be a dignified companion in the brilliant diplomatic career the ambassador was preparing for him.

Eduard, however, seemed more and more in love. Concerned, his mother went to talk to her husband.

'The art of diplomacy consists in keeping your opponent waiting,' said the ambassador. 'Whilst you may never get over a first love affair, it always ends.'

But Eduard seemed to have changed completely. He started bringing strange books home, he built a pyramid in his room, and, together with Maria, burned incense every night and spent hours staring at a strange design pinned on the wall. Eduard's marks at school began to get worse.

The mother didn't understand Portuguese, but she could see the book covers: crosses, bonfires, hanged witches, exotic symbols.

'Our son is reading some dangerous stuff.'

'Dangerous? What's happening in the Balkans is dangerous,' said the ambassador. 'There are rumours that Slovenia wants independence, and that could lead us into war.'

The mother, however, didn't care about politics; she wanted to know what was happening to her son.

'What about this mania for burning incense?'

'It's to disguise the smell of marijuana,' said the ambassador. 'Our son has had an excellent education, he can't possibly believe that those perfumed sticks draw down the spirits.'

'My son involved in drugs?'

'It happens. I smoked marijuana too when I was young; people soon get bored with it. I did.'

His wife felt proud and reassured. Her husband was an experienced man, he had entered the world of drugs and emerged unscathed. A man with such strength of will could control any situation.

One day, Eduard asked if he could have a bicycle.

'We've got a chauffeur and a Mercedes Benz. Why do you want a bicycle?'

'To be more in touch with nature. Maria and I are going on a ten-day trip,' he said. 'There's a place near here with huge deposits of crystal, and Maria says they give off really positive energy.'

His father and mother had been brought up under a communist regime: crystals were merely a mineral product composed of certain atoms, and did not give off any kind of energy, either positive or negative. They did some research and discovered that these ideas about 'crystal vibrations' were beginning to be fashionable.

If their son started talking about such things at official parties, he could appear ridiculous in the eyes of others. For the first time, the ambassador acknowledged that the situation was becoming serious. Brasília was a city that lived on rumours, and as soon as his rivals at the embassy learned that Eduard believed in these primitive superstitions, they might think he had picked them up from his parents, and diplomacy, as well as being the art of waiting, was also the art of keeping up a façade of normality whatever the circumstances.

'My boy, this can't go on,' said his father. 'I have friends in the Foreign Office in Yugoslavia. You have a brilliant career as a diplomat ahead of you and you've got to learn to face up to reality.'

Eduard left the house and didn't come back that night. His parents phoned Maria's house, as well as all the mortuaries and hospitals in the city, to no avail. The mother lost her confidence in her husband's abilities as head of the family, however good he might be at negotiating with complete strangers.

The following day, Eduard turned up, hungry and sleepy. He ate and went to his room, lit his incense sticks, said his mantras, and slept for the rest of that evening and night. When he woke up, a brand new bicycle was waiting for him.

'Go and see your crystals,' said his mother. 'I'll explain to your father.'

And so, on that dry, dusty afternoon, Edward cycled happily over to Maria's house. The city was so well designed (in the architects' opinion) or so badly designed (in Eduard's opinion), that there were almost no corners, he just kept straight on down a high speed lane, looking up at the sky full of rainless clouds, then he felt himself rising up at a tremendous speed towards the sky, only to plummet down again and land on the asphalt. Crash!

'I've had an accident.'

He tried to turn over, because his face was pressed against the asphalt, and realised he had no control over his own body. He heard the noise of cars braking, people talking in alarmed voices, someone approaching and trying to touch him, then a shout: 'Don't move him! If anyone moves him, he could be crippled for life!'

The seconds passed slowly and Eduard began to feel afraid. Unlike his parents, he believed in God and in the afterlife, but even so, it seemed grossly unfair to die at seventeen, staring at the asphalt, in a land not his own.

'Are you all right?' he heard someone say.

No, he wasn't all right, he couldn't move, but he couldn't say anything either. The worst thing was that he didn't lose consciousness, he knew exactly what was happening and what his situation was. Why didn't he faint? At precisely the moment when he was looking for God with such intensity, despite every-thing and everyone, God had no pity on him.

'The doctors are on their way,' someone whispered to him, clutching his hand. 'I don't know if you can hear me, but keep calm. It's nothing serious.'

Yes, he could hear, he would have liked that person – a man – to keep on talking, to promise him that it was nothing seri-ous, even though he was old enough to know that people only say that when the situation is very serious indeed. He thought about Maria, about the place where there were mountains of crystals full of positive energy, unlike Brasília, which had the highest concentration of negativity he had ever encountered in his meditations.

The seconds became minutes, people continued trying con-sole him, and for the first time since it all happened, he began to feel pain. A sharp pain that came from the centre of his head and seemed to spread throughout his entire body.

'They're here,' said the man who was holding his hand. 'Tomorrow you'll be riding your bike again.'

But the following day, Eduard was in hospital, with both his legs and one arm in plaster, unable to leave for at least a month, and having to listen to his mother's non-stop sobbing, his father's anxious phone calls and the doctor's reassurances, reit-erated every five minutes, that the crucial twenty-four hour period had passed, and there was no injury to the brain.

The family phoned the American Embassy, who never believed the diagnoses of the state hospitals and had their own sophisticated emergency service, along with a list of Brazilian doctors they considered capable of attending their own diplo-mats. Now and again, as part of a 'good neighbour policy', they allowed these services to be used by other diplomats.

The Americans brought along their state-of-the-art machines, carried out a further barrage of tests and examinations and reached the conclusion they always reach: the doctors in the state hospital had correctly evaluated the injuries and had taken the right decisions.

The doctors in the state hospital may have been good, but the programmes on Brazilian television were as awful as they are anywhere else in the world, and Eduard had little to do. Maria's visits to the hospital become more and more infrequent; perhaps she had found someone else to go with her to the crystal mountains.

In contrast to his girlfriend's erratic behaviour, the ambassador and his wife went to see him every day, but refused to bring him the Portuguese books he had at home on the pretext that his father would soon be transferred; so there was no need to learn a language he would never have to use again. Eduard, therefore, contented himself with talking to the other patients, discussing football with the nurses and devouring any magazines that fell into his hands.

Then one day, a nurse brought him a book he had just been given, but which he judged 'much too fat to actually read'. And that was the moment that Eduard's life began to set him on a strange path, one that would lead him to Villete and to his withdrawal from reality and that would distance him completely from all the things that other boys his age would get up to in the years that followed.

The book was about visionaries whose ideas had shaken the world, people with their own vision of an earthly Paradise, people who had spent their lives sharing their ideas with others. Jesus Christ was there, but so was Darwin and his theory that man was descended from the apes; Freud, affirming the importance of dreams; Columbus, pawning the Queen's jewels in order to set off in search of a new continent; Marx, with his belief that everyone deserved the same opportunities.

And there were saints too, like Ignatius Loyola, a Basque soldier who had slept with many women and killed many enemies in numerous battles, until he was wounded at Pamplona and came to understand the universe from the bed where he lay convalescing. Teresa of Ávila, who wanted somehow to find a path to God, and who stumbled across it when she happened to walk down a corridor and pause to look at a painting. Anthony, who, weary of the life he was leading, decided to go into exile in the desert, where he spent ten years in the company of demons and was racked by every conceivable temptation. Francis of Assisi, a young man like himself, who was determined to talk to the birds and to turn his back on everything that his parents had planned for his life.

Having nothing better to do, he began to read the 'fat book' that very afternoon. In the middle of the night, a nurse came in, asking if he needed help, since his was the only room with the light still on. Eduard waved her away, without even looking up from the book.

The men and women who shook the world were ordinary men and women, like him, like his father, like the girlfriend he knew he was losing. They were full of the same doubts and anxieties that all human beings experienced in their daily routine. They were people who had no special interest in religion or God, in expanding their minds or reaching a new level of consciousness, until one day they simply decided to change everything. The most interesting thing about the book was that it told how, in each of those lives, there was a single magical moment that made them set off in search of their own vision of Paradise.

They were people who had not allowed their lives to pass by blankly, and who, to achieve what they wanted, had begged for alms or courted kings, used diplomacy or force, flouted laws or faced the wrath of the powers-that-be, but who had never given up, and were always able to see the advantages in any difficulty that presented itself.

The following day, Eduard handed over his gold watch to the nurse who had given him the book, and asked him to sell it, and, with the money, to buy all the books he could find on the same subject. There weren't any more. He tried reading the biographies of some of those visionaries, but they were always described as if they were someone chosen, inspired, and not an ordinary person who, like everyone else, had to fight to be allowed to say what they thought.

Eduard was so impressed by what he had read, though, that he seriously considered becoming a saint and using the accident as an opportunity to change the direction of his life. But he had two broken legs, he had not had a single vision while in hospital, he hadn't stopped by a painting that shook him to his very soul, he had no friends who would build him a chapel in the middle of the Brazilian plateau, and the deserts were all far away and bristling with political problems. There was, however, something he could do: he could learn to paint and try to show the world the visions those men and women had experienced.

When they removed the plaster and he went back to the Embassy, surrounded by all the care, kindness and attention that the son of an ambassador could hope for from other diplomats, he asked his mother if he could enrol in a course on painting.

His mother said that he had already missed a lot of classes at the American school and that he would have to make up for lost time. Eduard refused. He did not have the slightest desire to go on learning about geography and sciences, he wanted to be a painter. In an unguarded moment, he explained why:

'I want to paint visions of Paradise.'

His mother said nothing, but promised to talk to her women friends and ascertain which was the best painting course available in the city.

When the ambassador came back from work that evening, he found her crying in her bedroom.

'Our son is mad,' she said, her face streaming with tears. 'The accident has affected his brain.'

'Impossible!' the ambassador replied, indignant. 'He was examined by doctors specially selected by the Americans.'

His wife told him what her son had said.

'It's just youthful rebelliousness. Just you wait, everything will go back to normal, you'll see.'

This time, waiting did no good at all, because Eduard was in a hurry to start living. Two days later, tired of marking time while his mother's friends deliberated, he decided to enrol himself on an art course. He started learning about colour and perspective, but he also got to know people who never talked about trainers or makes of car.

'He's living with artists!' said his mother tearfully to the ambassador.

'Oh, leave the boy alone,' said the ambassador. 'He'll soon get sick of it, like he did of his girlfriend, like he did of crystals, pyramids, incense and marijuana.'

But time passed, and Eduard's room became an improvised studio, full of paintings that made no sense at all to his parents:

circles, exotic colour combinations and primitive symbols all mixed up with people in attitudes of prayer.

Eduard, the solitary boy, who, in his two years in Brazil, had never once brought friends home, was now filling the house with strange people, all of them badly dressed and with untidy hair, who listened to horrible music at full blast – endlessly drinking and smoking and showing a complete disregard for basic good manners. One day, the director of the American school called his mother.

'I think your son must be involved in drugs,' she said. 'His school marks are well below average, and if he goes on like this, we won't be able to renew his enrolment.'

His mother went straight to the ambassador's office and told him what the director had said.

'You keep saying that, with time, everything will go back to normal,' she screamed hysterically. 'There's your crazy, drug-addict son, obviously suffering from some serious brain injury, and all you care about are cocktail parties and social gatherings.'

'Keep your voice down,' he said.

'No, I won't, and I never will again if you don't do something. The boy needs help, don't you see? Medical help. Do something.'

Concerned that the scene his wife was making might embarrass him in front of his staff, and worried that Eduard's interest in painting was lasting longer than expected, the ambassador, a practical man, who knew all the correct procedures, drew up a plan of attack.

First, he phoned his colleague, the American ambassador, and asked politely if he could again make use of the Embassy's medical facilities. His request was granted.

He went back to the accredited doctors, explained the situation and asked them to go over all the tests they had made at the time. The doctors, fearing a law suit, did exactly as they were asked and concluded that the tests revealed nothing abnormal. Before the ambassador left, they demanded that he sign a document exempting the American Embassy from any responsibility for sending him to them.

The ambassador immediately went to the hospital where Eduard had been a patient. He talked to the director, explained his son's problem and asked that, under the pretext of a routine checkup, a blood test be taken to see if there were any drugs in the boy's system.

They took a blood test and no trace of drugs was found.

There remained the third and final stage of his strategy: talking to Eduard himself and finding out what was going on. Only when he was in possession of all the facts, could he hope to make the correct decision.

Father and son sat down in the living room.

'Your mother's very worried about you,' said the ambassador. 'Your marks have got worse, and there's a danger that your place at the school won't be renewed.'

'But my marks at art school have improved, Dad.'

'I find your interest in art very pleasing, but you have your whole life ahead of you to do that. At the moment, the main thing is to finish your secondary education, so that I can set you on the path to a diplomatic career.'

Eduard thought long and hard before saying anything. He thought about the accident, about the book on visionaries, which had turned out to be only a pretext for finding his true vocation, and he thought about Maria, from whom he had never heard again. He hesitated for some time, but in the end, said:

'Dad, I don't want to be a diplomat. I want to be a painter.'

His father was prepared for that response and knew how to get round it.

'You will be a painter, but first, finish your studies. We'll arrange for exhibitions in Belgrade, Zagreb, Ljubljana and Sarajevo. I've got influence, I can help you a lot, but you must complete your studies.'

'If I do that, I'll be choosing the easy route. I'll enter some faculty or other, get a degree in a subject that doesn't interest me, but which will help me earn a living. Painting will just recede into the background, and I'll end up forgetting my vocation. I'll just have to find a way of earning money through my painting.'

The ambassador was starting to get irritated.

'You've got everything, son, a family which loves you, a house, money, social position, but as you know, our country is going through a difficult time, there are rumours of civil war. Tomorrow I might not even be here to help you.'

'I can help myself. Trust me. One day, I'll paint a series entitled "Visions of Paradise". It'll be a visual history of what men and women have previously only experienced in their hearts.'

The ambassador praised his son's determination, drew the conversation to a close with a smile, and decided to give him another month; after all, diplomacy is also the art of postponing decisions until the problems resolve themselves.

A month passed, and Eduard continued to devote all his time to painting, to his strange friends and to that music apparently expressly designed to induce some psychological disorder. To make matters worse, he had been expelled from the American college for arguing with a teacher about the existence of saints.

Since the decision could be put off no longer, the ambassador made one last attempt and called his son in for a man-to-man talk.

'Eduard, you are now of an age to take responsibility for your own life. We've put up with this for as long as we could, but now you've got to forget all this nonsense about becoming a painter and give some direction to your career.'

'But Dad, being a painter *is* giving a direction to my career.'

'What about our love for you, all our efforts to give you a good education. You never used to be like this, and I can only assume that what's happening is some consequence of the accident.'

'Look, I love you both more than anything or anyone else in the world.'

The ambassador cleared his throat. He wasn't used to such outspoken expressions of affection.

'Then, in the name of the love you have for us, please, do as your mother wants. Just stop all this painting business for a while, get some friends who belong to the same social class as you and go back to your studies.'

'You love me, Dad. You can't ask me to do that, because you've always set me a good example, fighting for the things you cared about. You can't want me to be a man with no will of my own.'

'I said, in the name of love. And I have never said that before, but I'm asking you now. For the love that you bear us, for the love we bear you, come home, and I don't just mean in the physical sense, but really. You're deceiving yourself, running away from reality.

'Ever since you were born, we've built up such dreams of how our lives would be. You're everything to us, our future and our past. Your grandfathers were civil servants and I had to fight like a lion to enter the diplomatic service and make my way up the ladder. And I did all this just to create a space for you, to make things easier for you. I've still got the pen with which I signed my first document as an ambassador, and I lovingly saved it to pass on to you the day you did the same.

'Don't let us down, son. We won't live forever and we want to die in peace, knowing that we've set you on the right path in life.

'If you really love us, do as I ask. If you don't love us, then carry on as you are now.'

Eduard sat for long hours staring up at the sky in Brasília, watching the clouds moving across the blue – beautiful clouds, but without a drop of rain in them to moisten the dry earth of the central Brazilian plateau. He was as empty as they were.

If he continued as he was, his mother would fade away with grief, his father would lose all enthusiasm for his career, and both would blame each other for failing in the upbringing of their beloved son. If he gave up his painting, the visions of Paradise would never see the light of day, and nothing else in this world could ever give him the same feelings of joy and pleasure.

He looked around him, he saw his paintings, he remembered the love and meaning he had put into each brushstroke, and he found every one of his paintings mediocre. He was a fraud, he wanted something for which he had not been chosen, and the price of which was his parents' disappointment.

Visions of Paradise were for the chosen few, who appeared in books as heroes and martyrs of the faith in which they believed, people who knew from childhood what the world wanted of them; the so-called facts in that first book he had read were the inventions of a storyteller.

At supper time, he told his parents that they were right; it was just a youthful dream; his enthusiasm for painting had

PAULO COELHO

passed. His parents were pleased, his mother wept with joy and embraced her son, and everything went back to normal.

That night, the ambassador secretly commemorated his victory by opening a bottle of champagne which he drank alone. When he went to bed, his wife – for the first time in many months – was already sleeping peacefully.

The following day, they found Eduard's room in confusion, the paintings slashed and the boy sitting in a corner, gazing up at the sky. His mother embraced him, told him how much she loved him, but Eduard didn't respond.

He wanted nothing more to do with love, he was fed up with the whole business. He had thought that he could just give up and follow his father's advice, but he had advanced too far in his work; he had crossed the abyss that separates a man from his dream and now there was no going back.

He couldn't go forwards or back. It was easier just to leave the stage.

Eduard stayed on in Brazil for another five months, being treated by specialists, who diagnosed a rare form of schizophrenia, possibly the result of a bicycle accident. Then war broke out in Yugoslavia and the ambassador was hastily recalled. It was too problematic for the family to look after Eduard, and the only way out was to leave him in the newly opened hospital of Villete.

By the time Eduard had finished telling his story, it was dark and they were both shivering with cold.

'Let's go in,' he said. 'They'll be serving supper.'

'Whenever we went to see my grandmother when I was a child, I was always fascinated by one particular painting in her house. It showed a woman – Our Lady, as Catholics call her – standing poised above the world, with her hands outstretched to the Earth and with rays of light streaming from her fingertips.

What most intrigued me about the painting was that this lady was standing on a live snake. I said to my grandmother: "Isn't she afraid of the snake? Won't it bite her on the foot and kill her with its poison?"

My grandmother said: "According to the Bible, the snake brought Good and Evil to the Earth, and she is keeping both Good and Evil in check with her love.'

'What's that got to do with my story?'

'I've only known you a week, so it would be far too early for me to tell you that I love you, but since I probably won't live through the night, it would also be too late. But then the great madness of men and women is precisely that: love.

'You told me a love story. I honestly believe your parents wanted the best for you, but their love almost destroyed your life. If Our Lady, as she appeared in my grandmother's painting, was treading on a snake, that indicates that love has two faces.'

'I see what you mean,' said Eduard. 'I provoked the nurses into giving me the electric shock treatment, because you get me all mixed up. I can't say for sure what I feel, and love has already destroyed me once.'

'Don't be afraid. Today, I asked Dr Igor for permission to leave here and to choose a place where I can close my eyes for ever. But when I saw you being held down by the nurses, I realised what it was I wanted to be looking at when I left this world: your face. And I decided not to leave.

'While you were sleeping off the effects of the electric shock treatment, I had another heart attack, and I thought my time had come. I looked at your face and I tried to guess what your story was, and I prepared myself to die happy. But death didn't come, my heart survived yet again, perhaps because I'm still young.'

He looked down.

'Don't be embarrassed about being loved. I'm not asking you for anything, just let me love you and play the piano again tonight, just once more, if I still have the strength to do it. In exchange, I ask only one thing, if you hear anyone say that I'm dying, go straight to my ward. Let me have my wish.'

Eduard remained silent for a long time and Veronika thought he must have retreated once more into his separate world, from which he would not return for a long time.

Then, he looked at the mountains beyond the walls of Villete and said:

'If you want to leave, I can take you. Just give me time to grab a couple of jackets and some money. Then we'll go.'

'It won't last long, Eduard. You do know that.'

Eduard didn't reply. He went in and came back at once carrying two jackets.

'It will last an eternity, Veronika, longer than all the identical days and nights I've spent in here, constantly trying to forget those visions of Paradise. And I almost did forget them too, though it seems to me they're coming back.

'Come on, let's go. Mad people do mad things.'

That night, when they were all gathered together for supper, the inmates noticed four people were missing.

Zedka, who everyone knew had been released after a long period of treatment, Mari, who had probably gone to the cinema, as she often did, and Eduard, who had perhaps not recovered from the electric shock treatment. When they thought this, all the inmates felt afraid, and they began their supper in silence.

Finally, the girl with green eyes and brown hair was missing. The one whom they all knew would not see out the week.

No one spoke openly of death in Villete, but absences were noted, although everyone always tried to behave as if nothing had happened.

A rumour started to go from table to table. Some wept, because she had been so full of life and now she would be lying in the small mortuary behind the hospital. Only the most daring ever went there, even during daylight hours. It contained three marble tables and there was generally a new body on one of them, covered with a sheet.

Everyone knew that tonight Veronika would be there. Those who were truly insane soon forgot the presence, during that week, of another guest, who sometimes disturbed everyone's sleep playing the piano. A few, when they heard the news, felt rather sad, especially the nurses who had been with

Veronika during her time in the Intensive Care Unit, but the employees had been trained not to develop strong bonds with the patients, because some left, others died, and the great majority got steadily worse. Their sadness lasted a little longer, and then that too passed.

The vast majority of the inmates, however, heard the news, pretended to be shocked and sad, but actually felt relieved, because once more, the Exterminating Angel had passed over Villete and they had been spared.

When the Fraternity got together after supper, one member of the group gave them a message: Mari had not gone to the cinema, she had left never to return and had given him a note.

No one seemed to attach much importance to the matter: she had always seemed different, rather too mad, incapable of adapting to the ideal situation in which they all lived in Villete.

'Mari never understood how happy we are here,' said one of them. 'We are friends with common interests, we have a routine, sometimes we go out on trips together, invite lecturers here to talk about important matters, then we discuss their ideas. Our life has reached a perfect equilibrium, something that many people outside would love to achieve.'

'Not to mention the fact that, in Villete, we are protected from unemployment, the consequences of the war in Bosnia, from economic problems and violence,' said another. 'We have found harmony.'

'Mari left me this note,' said the one who had given them the news, holding up a sealed envelope. 'She asked me to read it out loud, as if she were saying goodbye to us all.'

The oldest member of the group opened the envelope and did as Mari had asked. He was tempted to stop halfway, but by then, it was too late, and so he read to the end.

'When I was still a young lawyer, I read some poems by an

180

English poet and something he said impressed me greatly: "Be like the fountain that overflows, not like the cistern that merely contains." I always thought he was wrong: it was dangerous to overflow, because we might end up flooding areas occupied by our loved ones and drowning them with our love and enthusiasm. All my life I did my best to be a cistern, never going beyond the limits of my inner walls.

'Then, for some reason I will never understand, I began suffering from panic attacks. I became the kind of person I had fought so hard to avoid becoming: I became a fountain that overflowed and flooded everything around me. The result was my internment in Villete.

'After I was cured, I returned to the cistern and I met all of you. Thank you for your friendship, for your affection and for many happy moments. We lived together like fish in an aquarium, contented because someone threw us food when we needed it, and we could, whenever we wanted to, see the world outside through the glass.

'But yesterday, because of a piano and a young woman who is probably dead by now, I learned something very important: life inside is exactly the same as life outside. Both there and here, people gather together in groups, they build their walls and allow nothing strange to trouble their mediocre existences. They do things because they're used to doing them, they study useless subjects, they have fun because they're supposed to have fun, and the rest of the world can go hang – let them sort themselves out. At the very most, they watch the news on television – as we often did – as confirmation of their happiness, in a world full of problems and injustices.

'What I'm saying is that the life of the Fraternity is exactly the same as the lives of almost everyone outside Villete, carefully avoiding all knowledge of what lies beyond the glass walls of the aquarium. For a long time, it was comforting and useful, but people change, and now I'm off in search of adventure, even though I'm sixty-five and fully aware of all the limitations that age can bring. I'm going to Bosnia. There are people waiting for me there. Although they don't yet know me, and I don't know them. But I'm sure I can be useful, and the danger of an adventure is worth a thousand days of ease and comfort.'

When he had finished reading the note, the members of the Fraternity all went to their rooms and wards, telling themselves that Mari had finally gone mad.

Eduard and Veronika chose the most expensive restaurant in Ljubljana, ordered the finest dishes and got drunk on three bottles of 1988 wine, one of the best vintages of the century. During supper, they did not once mention Villete or the past or the future.

'I like that story about the snake,' he said, filling her glass for the nth time. 'But your grandmother was too old to be able to interpret the story correctly.'

'Have a little respect for my grandmother, please!' roared Veronika drunkenly, making everyone in the restaurant turn round.

'A toast to this young woman's grandmother!' said Eduard, jumping to his feet. 'A toast to the grandmother of this madwoman sitting here before me, who is doubtless some escapee from Villete.'

People turned their attention back to their food, pretending that nothing was happening.

'A toast to my grandmother!' insisted Veronika.

The owner of the restaurant came to their table.

'Will you please behave!'

They went quiet for a few moments, but soon resumed their loud talking, their nonsensical remarks and inappropriate behaviour. The owner of the restaurant went back to their table, told them they didn't need to pay the bill, but they had to leave that instant.

'Think of the money we'll save on that exorbitantly expensive wine,' said Eduard. 'Let's leave before this gentleman changes his mind.'

But the man wasn't about to change his mind. He was already pulling at Veronika's chair, an apparently courteous gesture intended to get her out of the restaurant as quickly as possible.

They walked to the middle of the small square in the centre of the city. Veronika looked up at her convent room and her drunkenness vanished. She remembered that soon she would die.

'Let's buy some more wine!' said Eduard.

There was a bar nearby. Eduard bought two bottles and the two of them sat down and continued drinking.

'What's wrong with my grandmother's interpretation of the painting?' said Veronika.

Eduard was so drunk that he had to make an immense effort to remember what he had said in the restaurant, but he managed it.

'Your grandmother said that the woman was standing on the snake because love must master Good and Evil. It's a nice, romantic interpretation, but it's nothing to do with that. I've seen that image before, it's one of the visions of Paradise I imagined painting. I used to wonder why they always depicted the Virgin like that.'

'And why do they?'

'Because the Virgin equals female energy and is the mistress of the snake, which signifies wisdom. If you look at the ring Dr Igor wears, you'll see that it bears the physician's symbol: two serpents coiled around a stick. Love is above wisdom, just as the Virgin is above the snake. For her, everything is Inspiration. She doesn't bother judging what is Good and what Evil.'

'Do you know something else?' said Veronika. 'The Virgin never took any notice of what others might think of her. Imagine having to explain to everyone that business about the Holy Ghost. She didn't explain anything, she just said: "That's what happened." And do you know what the others must have said?'

'Of course. That she was mad.'

They both laughed. Veronika raised her glass.

'Congratulations. You should paint those visions of Paradise, rather than just talking about them.'

'I'll begin with you,' said Eduard.

Beside the small square there is a small hill. On top of the small hill, there is a small castle. Veronika and Eduard trudged up the steep path, cursing and laughing, slipping on the ice and complaining of exhaustion.

Beside the castle, there is a gigantic yellow crane. For anyone coming to Ljubljana for the first time, the crane gives the impression that the castle is being restored and that work will soon be completed. The inhabitants of Ljubljana, however, know that the crane has been there for many years, although no one knows why. Veronika told Eduard that when children in kindergarten are asked to draw the castle of Ljubljana, they always include the crane in the drawing.

'Besides, the crane is much better preserved than the castle.'

Eduard laughed.

'You should be dead by now,' he said, still under the effects of alcohol, but with a flicker of fear in his voice. 'Your heart shouldn't have survived that climb.'

Veronika gave him a long, lingering kiss.

'Look at my face,' she said. 'Remember it with the eyes of your soul, so that you can reproduce it one day. If you like, that can be your starting point, but you must go back to painting.

That is my last request. Do you believe in God?'

'I do.'

'Then you must swear by the God you believe in that you will paint me.'

'I swear.'

'And that after painting me, you will go on painting.'

'I don't know if I can swear that.'

'You can. And I'll go further: thank you for giving meaning to my life. I came into this world in order to go through everything I've gone through, attempted suicide, ruining my heart, meeting you, coming up to this castle, letting you engrave my face on your soul. That is the only reason I came into the world, to make you go back to the path you strayed from. Don't make me feel my life has been in vain.'

'I don't know if it's too early or too late, but, just as you did with me, I want to tell you that I love you. You don't have to believe it, maybe it's just foolishness, a fantasy of mine.'

Veronika put her arms around him and asked the God she did not believe in to take her at that very moment.

She closed her eyes and felt him doing the same. And a deep dreamless sleep came upon her. Death was sweet, it smelled of wine and it stroked her hair.

Eduard felt someone prodding him in the shoulder. When he opened his eyes, day was breaking.

'You can go and shelter in the Town Hall, if you like,' said the policeman. 'You'll freeze if you stay here.'

In a second, Eduard remembered everything that had happened the previous night. There was a woman lying curled in his arms.

'She ... she's dead.'

But the woman moved and opened her eyes.

'What's going on?' asked Veronika.

'Nothing,' said Eduard, helping her to her feet. 'Or rather, a miracle happened: another day of life.'

As soon as Dr Igor went into his consulting room and turned on the light – for daylight still arrived late and winter was dragging on far too long – a nurse knocked at his door.

'Things have started early today,' he said to himself.

It was going to be a difficult day, because of the conversation he would have to have with Veronika. He had been building up to it all week, and had hardly slept a wink the previous night.

'I've got some worrying news,' said the nurse. 'Two of the inmates have disappeared: the ambassador's son and the girl with the heart problem.'

'Honestly, you're a load of incompetents, you are, not that the security in this hospital has ever been up to much.'

'It's just that no one's ever tried to escape before,' said the nurse, frightened. 'We didn't know it was possible.'

'Get out of here! Now I'll have to prepare a report for the owners, notify the police, take steps. Tell everyone I'm not to be disturbed, these things take hours!'

The nurse left, looking pale, knowing that a large part of that major problem would land on his own shoulders, because that is how the powerful deal with the weak. He would doubtless be dismissed before the day was out.

Dr Igor picked up a pad, put it on the table and began making notes; then he changed his mind.

He switched off the light and sat in the office precariously lit by the incipient sunlight, and he smiled. It had worked.

In a while, he would make the necessary notes, describing the only known cure for Vitriol: an awareness of life. And describing the medication he had used in his first major test on patients: an awareness of death.

Perhaps other forms of medication existed, but Dr Igor had decided to centre his thesis round the one he had the opportunity to experiment with scientifically, thanks to a young woman who, quite unwittingly, had become part of his fate. She had been in a terrible state when she arrived, suffering from a severe overdose, nearly in a coma. She had hovered between life and death for nearly a week, just the amount of time he needed to come up with a brilliant idea for his experiment.

Everything depended on one thing: the girl's capacity to survive.

And she had, with no serious consequences, no irreversible health problems; if she looked after herself, she could live as long or longer than him.

But Dr Igor was the only one who knew this, just as he knew that failed suicides tend to repeat the attempt sooner or later. Why not use her as a guinea pig, to see if he could eliminate the Vitriol, or Bitterness, from her organism?

And so Dr Igor had conceived his plan.

Using a drug known as Fenotal, he had managed to simulate the effects of heart attacks. For a week, she had received injections of the drug, and she must have been very frightened, because she had time to think about death and to review her own life. In that way, according to Dr Igor's thesis (the final chapter of his work would be entitled 'An awareness of death encourages us to live more intensely') the girl had gone on to eliminate Vitriol completely from her organism, and would, quite possibly, never repeat her attempt at suicide.

He was supposed to see her today and tell her that, thanks to the injections, he had achieved a total reversal of her heart condition. Veronika's escape saved him the unpleasant experience of lying to her yet again.

What Dr Igor had not counted on was the infectious nature of his cure for Vitriol poisoning. A lot of people in Villete had been frightened by their awareness of that slow, irreparable death. They must all have been thinking about what they were missing, forced to re-evaluate their own lives.

Mari had come to him asking to be discharged. Other patients were asking for their cases to be reviewed. The position of the ambassador's son was more worrying, though, because he had simply disappeared, probably helping Veronika to escape.

'Perhaps they're still together,' he thought.

At any rate, the ambassador's son knew where Villete was, if he wanted to come back. Dr Igor was too excited by the results to pay much attention to minor details.

For a few moments, he was assailed by another doubt: sooner or later, Veronika would realise that she wasn't going to die of a heart attack. She would probably go to a specialist who would tell her that her heart was perfectly normal. She would judge that the doctor who had taken care of her in Villete was a complete incompetent, but then all those who dare to research into forbidden subjects require both a certain amount of courage and a good dose of incomprehension.

But what about the many days that she would have to live with the fear of imminent death?

Dr Igor pondered the arguments long and hard and decided that it didn't really matter. She would consider each day a miracle, which indeed it is, when you consider the number of unexpected things that could happen in each second of our fragile existences.

He noticed that the sun's rays were growing stronger; at that hour, the inmates would be having breakfast. Soon his waiting room would be full, the usual problems would arise, and it was best to start taking notes at once for his thesis.

Meticulously he began to write up his experiment with Veronika; he would leave until later the reports on the building's lack of security.

St Bernadette's Day, 1998

THE ALCHEMIST
Paulo Coelho

Every few decades a book is published that changes the lives of the readers forever. Paulo Coelho's *The Alchemist* is such a book. With over 20 million copies sold worldwide, *The Alchemist* has already achieved the status of a modern classic.

This is the magical story of Santiago, an Andalusian shepherd boy who yearns to travel in search of a worldly treasure as extravagant as any ever found. From his home in Spain he journeys to the markets of Tangiers and into the Egyptian desert, where a fateful encounter with the alchemist awaits him.

This story teaches us, as only few can, about the essential wisdom of listening to our hearts, learning to read the omens strewn along life's path and above all about following our dreams.

THE FIFTH MOUNTAIN
Paulo Coelho

Fleeing his home from persecution 23-year-old Elijah takes refuge with a young widow and her son in the beautiful town of Akbar. Already struggling to maintain his sanity in a chaotic world of tyranny and war, he is now forced to choose between his new-found love and his overwhelming sense of duty.

Evoking all the drama and intrigue of the colourful, chaotic world of the Middle East, Paulo Coelho turns the trials of Elijah into an intensely moving and inspiring story – one that powerfully brings out the universal themes of how faith and love can ultimately triumph over suffering.

THE VALKYRIES
Paulo Coelho

From Paulo Coelho, author of the international best-seller *The Alchemist*, comes the true record of an exotic odyssey, a profound work to enchant and thrill the reader.

Haunted by a devastating curse, Paulo is instructed by his mysterious spiritual teacher to embark upon a journey to find and speak to his guardian angel in an attempt to confront and overcome his dark past. *The Valkyries* is a compelling account of this journey which takes him, with his wife Chris, on a forty day quest into the searing heat of the Mojave Desert.

At once a modern-day adventure, a metaphysical battle with self-doubt and fear, and a true story of two people striving to understand one another, *The Valkyries* is ultimately a story about forgiving our past and believing our future.

BY THE RIVER PIEDRA
I SAT DOWN AND WEPT
Paulo Coelho

By *The River Piedra* tells the story of Pilar, an independent and practical yet restless young woman, who is frustrated by the daily grind of university life and looking for greater meaning in her life. Pilar is transformed forever by an encounter with a childhood friend, now a mesmerizing and handsome spiritual teacher – and a rumoured miracle worker – who leads her on a journey through the French Pyrenees, a magical landscape that has been home to holy visions and miracles through the ages.

THE PILGRIMAGE
Paulo Coelho

The Pilgrimage recounts the spectacular trials of Paulo Coelho and his mysterious mentor, Petrus, as they journey across Spain in search of a miraculous sword, on a legendary road travelling by pilgrims of San Tiago since the Middle Ages. Part adventure story, part guide to self-mastery, this compelling tale delivers a powerful brew of magic and insight.